BEWARE THE LAUGHING GULL

A Lucy Wayles Mystery

Lydia Adamson

A SIGNET BOOK

SIGNET
Published by the Penguin Group
Penguin Putnam Inc., 375 Hudson Street,
New York, New York 10014, U.S.A.
Penguin Books Ltd, 27 Wrights Lane,
London W8 5TZ, England
Penguin Books Australia Ltd, Ringwood,
Victoria, Australia
Penguin Books Canada Ltd, 10 Alcorn Avenue,
Toronto, Ontario, Canada M4V 3B2
Penguin Books (N.Z.) Ltd, 182-190 Wairau Road,
Auckland 10, New Zealand

Penguin Books Ltd, Registered Offices:
Harmondsworth, Middlesex, England

First published by Signet, an imprint of Dutton NAL,
a member of Penguin Putnam Inc.

First Printing, August, 1998
10 9 8 7 6 5 4 3 2 1

ELEMENTARY, MY DEAR BIRD-WATCHERS

Lucy declared grandly, "I have assembled you here because it is time, I believe, to resurrect the investigative apparatus of Olmsted's Irregulars."

New members Isobel and Timothy looked confused. They didn't know that Olmsted's Irregulars were really a clone of the Baker Street Irregulars. They thought we were strictly a bird-watching group.

"What, precisely, is to be investigated?" John Wu inquired.

Lucy's answering sigh seemed to encompass the four sides of the apartment, indeed the world.

"I do believe our dear friend Peter Marin is caught in a web of violence and duplicity from which he will not emerge—alive—without our help. I also do believe that the moment we can identify the shape of the web strangling poor Peter we will know why his bride was murdered and by whom."

Chapter 1

My father, may he rest in peace, used to say that there are three topics that should never be brought up at dinner. Or breakfast or lunch for that matter: sex, politics, and religion.

He left out birds.

Predictably, it was the subject of birds that started the argument on that very warm August morning.

It was about ten-thirty.

We—and by "we" I mean the Olmsted's Irregulars—had just spent three hours or so bird-watching in the Ramble, that thickly wooded gem in Central Park.

There were six of us—

Lucy Wayles, the founder, spiritual adviser, and master sergeant of our group.

Peter Marin, a charter member, a large red-haired man who, though he dresses and looks like a bearded Li'l Abner, is in fact a successful and highly regarded commercial artist with an astonishing triplex apartment.

John Wu, another charter member, slim and fastidious, an investment counselor who lives and dies by his laptop, on which he accomplishes all kinds of byzantine trading and the mysterious manipulation of even more mysterious data.

Myself, Markus Bloch, also a charter member. I am a retired M.D.—a medical researcher known primarily as the man who loves Lucy Wayles and follows her about like Sancho Panza.

Two of our number are new to the group, making up for the departure of the lovely Willa Wayne, who had to leave us when her husband, a violinist with the New York Philharmonic, secured a second chair position with the Cleveland Orchestra.

Timothy (last name not revealed) is a tall, gangly, excruciatingly shy young black man with the largest feet I have ever seen on a human. He is a science fiction writer, a waiter by night, and a diligent birder. We all like Timothy, but once in a while he behaves in a peculiar fashion. He is constantly becoming perplexed about arcane matters that have nothing to do with the matter at hand—i.e., bird-watching. You might be next to him in a glade, binoculars raised, and you'll hear him mutter something like, "I cannot *believe* that there are really seven thousand islands in the Philippines."

The second new member is Isobel Soba, a jolly, heavyset former Maryknoll nun who now teaches in the graduate center of Fordham University. Lucy, when she was still director of the Library of Urban Natural History (since absorbed by the Museum of Natural History), had met Isobel at some kind of professional gathering and suggested that she join a bird-watching group. So she did, belatedly. Isobel has a few personal quirks—habits, problems, however you'd like to put it—that the rest of the group found difficult to bear at first. She smokes, for one; in fact, she chain-smokes an evil-smelling low tar menthol cigarette. She is also the only birder I have ever come across who, in the summer, goes birding with a portable ice chest to hold her cans of beer. She favors a strange imported brew, unknown to me, and she seems to consume it by the barrel. But all that was soon overcome, since she is a joy to be with. The one lingering area of mistrust vis-à-vis Isobel was a troubling rumor that she was a tree hugger . . . that she was seen hugging a European beech just past the Bow Bridge. But Lucy assured us that if indeed Isobel was a tree hugger, she was not the kind that hated woodpeckers.

So, that is the cast of characters, so to speak.

Now, let me get to the argument.

We were all weary when we climbed down the small gully where we always took our repast. Quickly, out came the hard-boiled eggs and the oranges and the bottles of spring water.

It had been a very busy morning for bird-watchers. The late summer migration out of the park was starting. The social birds were restless . . . always moving . . . gathering into flocks. The solitaries seemed to be praying.

At one point early on in the morning—we were in the Ramble at the time—John Wu had casually announced that he had spotted a yellow-breasted chat.

"Where?" Lucy asked, in that throaty whisper all serious birders cultivate.

"Over there, in the brush, behind the stone

arch. But he's gone," John said. And the sighting was forgotten even though it is rare to see a yellow-breasted chat in Central Park.

It was not until some hours later, as we were resting and eating, that Isobel, one of the new Irregulars, said rather sternly to John, "Are you sure it was a yellow-breasted chat you saw?"

All the old-timers tensed. Of all the wrong things you might say to John Wu, challenging one of his pronouncements was about the "wrongest" you could possibly get.

John continued with the peeling of his second hard-boiled egg, finishing the task before he responded to Isobel with an arch "Excuse me?"

Isobel lit one of her cigarettes and blew the smoke skyward. "Well, all I'm saying is that it's odd that no one else saw it. We were all bunched together."

"The bird was skulking," John explained.

For some reason Isobel found this very funny. She burst out laughing at the talk of the skulking bird.

John opened a napkin, laid it on the grass, placed the stripped egg on the napkin, and stared at the new member of the group. I experienced a small but measurable shudder of fear. I looked to Lucy for help or corroboration. She seemed uninterested. She seemed, in fact, utterly absorbed in her orange, having done with the peeling and now moving on to sectioning it. I sighed. Everything about that woman fascinated me. Even the way she peeled an orange. That, dear children, is love among the older set. It has its own peculiarities.

But then I caught her giving John Wu a quick, ever so quick and anxious glance. As head of the Olmsted's Irregulars, she knew her troops as well as she knew the park's birds, and sometimes John Wu spiraled out of control.

"My dear lady," John Wu said, lapsing into the kind of formal address that was an unmistakable signal of his irritation, "the yellow-breasted chat is one of the largest of the warblers. It has many unwarblerlike characteristics . . . such as singing like a mockingbird. It does not really behave or look like a warbler at all. But it *is* one. I assure you I know it when I see it. And I saw it skulking in the Ramble."

Miss Isobel Soba listened, grinned, popped a can of her strange beer, and went into a Tallulah imitation: "Dahling! If you say chat . . . I say chat." She then began to puff furiously at her cigarette, drawing in and blowing out absurd amounts of smoke and holding on to the filter tip as if it were one of those vampish, bejeweled holders from the 1920s.

This really infuriated John, but before he could retaliate, Peter Marin said the three little words that ended the argument.

"I'm getting married," he announced.

There was stunned silence.

"The day after tomorrow," Peter continued. "Right here. Where we are now standing—or sitting, as the case may be. And you're all invited. There'll be a party at my place afterward—just for the Olmsted's Irregulars—and there'll be more good food than you ever saw in you life. And two bands. And hand-dipped ice cream from . . . from . . . well, somewhere in New Jersey, with a barrel of crushed walnuts in syrup."

"Congratulations, Peter," Lucy said firmly. Then added, "Would it be possible to find out whom you are marrying before the ceremony?"

"Oh, yes, indeed! Her name is Teresa Aguilar. And she is the most beautiful and intelligent and exciting woman I have ever met. You will all love her. And she'll love you."

All kinds of cryptic glances were being thrown

about. Because those who knew Peter Marin knew that when it came to women, he was a demented middle-aged bachelor. He fell in and out of love with great rapidity and great intensity—virtually always with the most inappropriate partners, such as fanatical cult members or cross dressers.

Lucy asked sweetly, "Do I know her, Peter?"

"I don't think so. I just didn't bring her around. But once we're married you'll see her all the time. She loves the park. She loves birds. She loves people."

Peter thumped the ground beside him. "And—can you imagine?—we have decided to get married right here."

Timothy, who was stretched out on the grass, feet toward the small rivulet that bisected the gully, offered Peter one of his peanut butter crackers. Peter waved it off.

"I thought it would be perfect. Come as you are. We finish birding for the morning and then we just have a wedding. Mine. Lucy! Don't you think it's a brilliant idea?"

"Brilliant!" Lucy agreed.

"Rain or shine," Peter said. "Two days from now. Right here. Same time, same station. It will be as if nothing was planned. Like a good sketch book."

The skulking yellow-breasted chat was now only a dim memory.

I took out my black plastic Glad bag—entrusted to me because I was official garbage person for the Olmsted's Irregulars—and began a preliminary cleanup.

I could hear John Wu telling Peter that he should reconsider this marital step. "I don't believe you have thought it through," he was saying.

When Isobel Soba said, "Amen!" John gave her a dirty look. She blew smoke at him. I took a misstep and a spasm of pain shot through my lower back. I yelped, turned and groaned. Lucy was looking at me with concern.

I smiled to show her it was just a twinge. She smiled back. My heart fair to burst to see my true love so lovely and so regal and so compassionate in that gully. Oh, Lucy Wayles . . . she had that kind of severe mature beauty leavened with a smidgen of depravity . . . if I may use that word.

Then Lucy did a very strange thing. She winked at me. I had no idea what it meant. So I just went back to my assignment and completed it to the best of my ability.

The funny thing was, it happened just as Peter Marin said it would happen and it didn't seem strange at all.

Furthermore, from the time Peter announced it to the time the actual event commenced . . . nobody even spoke about it.

No doubt, most of us didn't think it would happen. This was not the first time Peter Marin had announced wedding plans.

But there we were. In the gully again, resting, peeling hard-boiled eggs and oranges.

It was a cooler and darker morning and the birding had been poor.

Everyone, including Peter, was dressed in the usual manner for a field trip.

Then . . . what a transformation.

A beautiful woman in a white dress with a white shawl appeared on the rim of the gully.

Accompanying her, his arm carefully linked with hers, was a kindly looking man in a brown suit. Last, there was a younger man carrying a collapsible table and several bottles of champagne.

Timothy whispered to me, "We have now reached one of the outermost planets in the galaxy."

Teresa Aguilar, Peter Marin's intended, made her way down the slope. As crazy as the unfolding scene was, I felt a sudden and bitter pang of jealousy. If only that were Lucy Wayles coming down that slope to take my hand . . . "to be joined forever in the bosom of the Lord," as her mad old Aunt Hattie would say (forgive me, Spinoza).

Peter guided his beloved around the gully, introducing her to each of the Olmsted's Irregulars.

She was a small, sweet-looking thing, very slim, with one of those swanlike Spanish necks. Her jet-black hair was cut short, and the white shawl around her shoulders combined with the white dress made her seem like an angel sent down from above on some specially lovely mission.

When the champagne bottles were judiciously lined up for the eventual uncorking, and the brown-suited gentleman, who, Peter told us, was a Unitarian minister, had taken his place behind the now opened table—we all knew this was no joke. This *was* a marriage. Peter Marin was really about to get married.

They made a very odd couple as they approached the table.

She, so young and so beautiful and so elegant.

He, so burly and crazed-looking in his Li'l Abner coveralls and his red beard.

I said to Lucy, "He certainly picked a beautiful young lady to marry."

For some odd reason this comment irked her. I could tell she was irked because she started to snap the old hippie headband that she always wore when birding. And then, as if to prove beyond a shadow of a doubt that she was indeed angry at my innocent remark, she flipped her binocular case shut.

"Dear, sweet Markus," she said with a kind of indulgent sigh. Oh, dear. This down-home lead-in invariably signaled that some pointed, often barbed comment was to follow. "Dear, sweet Markus," she repeated, "remember the white-eared hummingbird."

She patted my arm for emphasis.

Oh, no. Another one of her infuriating cryptic sayings.

"What does that mean, Lucy?" I demanded in

a hushed whisper, my eyes on the bride and groom.

"Leks," said John Wu.

"What?" I said.

"Is that a soup?" Isobel Soba queried.

"No!" snapped John. "A lek is a site on which male birds display communally to attract females. The white-eared hummingbird males sing altogether. The female struts by and chooses the one who sings best, then leads him away to mate."

"But, Lucy," I said, "Peter Marin's voice is even worse than mine."

Lucy gave me a withering look. Obviously I had, once again, missed the point.

Isobel hushed us. The ceremony was about to begin.

The minister placed a tooled leather Bible on the table along with two gold rings.

He looked benevolently at the bride and groom; he looked out at the guests.

"We are about to embark on what is, in my opinion, the most sacred ritual in Christendom," he said. "The binding of two souls in holy matrimony."

He paused thoughtfully then. "Did it ever

occur to you why the harsh word 'binding'—
which has its Old Testament origins in the binding of Isaac for sacrifice—is also used for the
marriage ceremony?"

He began to explain.

But a sudden shout from above stopped him.

A roller blader on the West Drive had obviously gotten into difficulty, lost control, jumped
the small barrier, and was now hurtling down
the gully toward us.

The young skater, a long-haired blond, was
holding on to his helmet with both hands and
screaming out warnings.

The grass gully slowed the roller blader down
and he stumbled to a halt right beside the minister's table.

He pulled the helmet off and laughed heartily.
We all joined in the laughter.

He pointed to the Bible on the table. "Divine
intervention," he said, obviously in explanation
of his miraculous trip down the gully, unscathed
and standing.

Indeed, we were still laughing when he pulled
a small, smoke-gray handgun from inside his
helmet, pressed it flush against the bride's tem-
ple, and pulled the trigger.

The sound of death is paralyzing. It was impossible to move. We might have all been rocks.

Teresa Aguilar fell over the table.

The roller blader kicked off his skates, tucked them under his arm, ran up the slope, and vaulted over the wall onto Central Park West.

I could clearly see the Bible stained with the bride's blood and gore.

For some reason, two thoughts crossed my mind.

The first one was irrational: I recalled that the title of Edmund Wilson's great work on the Civil War—*Patriotic Gore*—came from the song "Oh, Maryland, My Maryland."

The second thought was quite rational. Pity, I said to myself, there'll be no wedding this morning.

Chapter 2

"Why didn't you do something?" young Timothy asked me as they were taking the gravely wounded young woman up the slope.

"What could I do?"

"I mean, you are a physician . . . aren't you?"

"Retired. And I never really practiced," I said. But he was right. The shooting had absolutely paralyzed my will except for a few quaint, irrelevant thoughts. It was the minister who had attempted to stop the bleeding.

I saw Lucy escorting Peter Marin up the slope. "We're going to the hospital," she called back to me. Peter was still dazed. He walked like a zombie.

Around us there was orchestrated chaos. EMS vehicles, police cars, uniformed officers stringing yellow crime-scene ribbons—and hundreds of walkers, bikers, bladers staring down at us from the West Drive.

Two homicide detectives were interrogating John Wu, scribbling in their pads as they proceeded.

Then they came to me. Their names were, if I remember correctly, Detective Isaac Rupp and Detective Jack Halkin. They seemed to be concentrating on obtaining a description of the shooter. All I remembered was that he had long yellow hair and was on roller blades.

When pressed by Rupp, who seemed to me a bit unfriendly, I recalled the words that murderous young man had spoken: "Divine intervention." It had been meant as a macabre joke, I presumed.

They asked me a few questions about myself, personal questions, and my relationship to the groom. And that was that.

They moved on to Timothy. I could see that these constables, if I may use that archaic term, were becoming crankier and crankier.

Obviously they were expecting more clarity and precision from bird-watchers. I knew what they were thinking: How come these people, who can identify a tiny, swiftly moving object from two hundred yards away in dense brush, cannot give us a clear description of a young man who was, at most, five feet from each of them.

Being a man of reason, I would have solved this paradox for them elegantly if they had asked me. Yes, bird-watchers are sharp-eyed. But they are *looking* for birds. No one was looking for a murderer on roller blades at a wedding.

Then I heard a strange grumbling nearby. It was Isobel. She was seated yogilike on the grass in a cloud of smoke. She was definitely talking to herself.

"Are you okay?" I asked gently, ever the gallant.

She looked up. "Do you know why I drink so much beer?" she asked.

"No."

"I find it the best of all heartburn medicines."

"Well," I replied, "to each his own. I prefer Mylanta."

"And I require such a medicine because I habitually overeat. Do you want to know why I overeat, Markus?"

"If you wish to tell me."

"I do, but I simply can't disclose why at this time. We simply don't know each other well enough yet. But I will tell you this . . ."

She stood up and pointed a finger at her own chest, as if she were declaring something of importance. "*They* can beat me . . . torture me . . . loose all the hounds of hell upon me . . . but I shall never confess."

"Now, now, Isobel. They just want to ask you a few questions," I replied, wondering why she was getting so worked up just because the two detectives were approaching to speak to her.

She moved closer to me and whispered, "He never saw a yellow-breasted chat in those bushes."

Ah well, I thought, bird-watchers will be bird-watchers.

I didn't get back to my gloomy apartment on far West Fifty-seventh Street until two in the afternoon.

And the moment I walked inside I knew there was more trouble afoot. Strange sounds were emanating from my bedroom.

I peeked in. What a horrific sight! Duke was on my bed. He had selected both pairs of my dress shoes from the closet and dragged them onto the bed and was now calmly chewing the plastic tips off the laces. These were my only "good" shoes—reserved for funerals, state dinners, and the like. These were my Madison Avenue shoes, purchased at one hundred and sixty-five dollars a pair. One black pair, one brown.

I didn't know what to do.

Duke is the small, dun-colored, ugly, three-legged pit bull foisted on me by Lucy Wayles.

I am afraid of pit bulls in general and Duke in particular. But I had thought we had reached a kind of live and let live plateau. He had his own room. I fed him and walked him and in exchange he never mauled me.

Of course I was always leery, particularly after I contacted several dog-walking services and they all refused to enroll Duke, even when I threatened them with a lawsuit under the Americans for Disabilities Act, or whatever it is called. Whether or not their refusals were based on his three-leggedness, or on the bad reputation of the breed—I didn't know. Did it matter?

Now there he was . . . in *my* bedroom . . . on

my bed . . . chewing up about three hundred and fifty dollars of my leather.

He looked at me slyly with his ferocious beady eyes. Obviously he was quite happy to announce that the social contract between us had been suspended.

Worse, I knew he knew I was afraid of him. And why shouldn't I be? According to Lucy, he had lost his leg in a DEA shootout in Queens involving his late owner, a drug dealer. The man was killed. The drugs confiscated. The dog wounded and placed in a shelter.

My first instinct was to reason with him. I said, in a very modulated and articulated speech pattern: "Duke.Those are my dress shoes. Can't you select the tennis shoes instead? There is no difference in taste or nutritional value between dress shoe lace tips and sneaker lace tips."

He gave me one of those "I'm a pit bull" looks, cocking his head, and a thuggish head it was, ever so slightly, narrowing the eyes, scrunching down a bit.

My second impulse was to call Lucy. She'd know how to handle him. She always did. But Lucy was at the hospital with Peter Marin, at the bedside of his bride.

So I went into the kitchen, poured some ginger ale, took the glass into the living room, sat down on the chair to devise a strategy—and promptly fell asleep.

At five o'clock a noise woke me. It was Duke. He had hobbled into the living room with just one of my shoes and was shredding it on the carpet, not five feet from me. This time it wasn't the lace tips—it was the shoe itself.

"You are a vindictive animal," I said to him and for a moment I thought of several ruses that would enable me to steal the shoe back safely. Then I realized that my once demonstrable quickness of hand and foot had vanished several years back. Such a ruse might put me squarely in harm's way.

Stymied, I turned on the television news.

The feature story was the shooting in Central Park.

And the news was all bad.

Teresa Aguilar had died at three-thirty in the afternoon at St. Luke's Hospital.

Peter Marin had been issued a summons for conducting a wedding in the park without a permit.

The police had no suspects in custody at this time.

The announcer then went on to give a brief description of the assassin: white male about twenty-five with long blond hair on roller blades with full accoutrements: i.e., helmet, lycra suit, elbow pads, etc.

Then the announcer said, "One of the guests at this wedding was a woman whom the NYPD is quite familiar with—Lucy Wayles."

I sat up, astonished.

Then on the screen flashed that three-year-old video footage of Lucy being arrested after she had rescued a frozen tufted duck from a girder high up on the Fifty-ninth Street Bridge and tied up the city's vehicular traffic for five hours.

It was this arrest that had caused Lucy to be ejected from the main Central Park bird-watchers group, whereupon she formed the rogue group: Olmsted's Irregulars.

The telephone rang. I shut the set off. It was Lucy.

"Did you hear the bad news, Markus?"

"Yes. Just now. On the TV. How is Peter?"

"As well as can be expected. Which means not good at all. I think it is necessary that the Irregulars meet as usual tomorrow morning and make sure Peter is with us."

"Yes. A good idea. A therapeutic intervention."

"Get some sleep, Markus."

"Wait, Lucy. Don't hang up."

"What?"

"I'm having trouble with Duke."

"Is he ill?"

"No. He's destroying my dress shoes—chewing them up."

"Markus, remember what I told you this morning, before the tragedy?"

"Oh, you mean about the white-eared hummingbird."

"No. About the laughing gull."

"Lucy, I remember it distinctly. You told me, in exactly the following words: Beware the white-eared hummingbird."

"No, I said beware the laughing gull."

"I don't want to argue with you, Lucy. I want your help now with Duke."

"Of course I'll help you, Markus. Is there anyone dearer to me than you? Tell me: Do you know why the gull laughs?"

"No."

"Because it can't sing."

I didn't get it.

Lucy hung up. I looked at Duke. He had fallen asleep over the shoe. I tiptoed past him to retrieve and hide the others.

Chapter 3

We gathered as usual at the foot of the John Puroy Mitchell statue, just inside the park at East Ninetieth Street.

I arrived at 6:55 A.M. Lucy and John Wu were already there. Isobel Soba arrived at seven sharp, and Timothy, breathlessly, two minutes later. He apologized profusely for being late, explaining that he had missed his stop on the bus because he was so engrossed in the new revelatory biography of Einstein.

We waited in silence for Peter. I was quite happy. After all, Lucy was there—tall, thin, beautiful, imperturbable, giving me a smile once in a while.

She wore what she always wore when birding: her worn old barn jacket, corduroy slacks, and a gaily colored headband. She carried her trusty knapsack and wore cut-down construction boots with thick soles. Around her neck were the small waterproof Leica binoculars she prized.

And still we waited for Peter. At ten minutes past seven John Wu announced, "It's time to go. There have been rumors about a double-crested cormorant at the southwest quadrant of the reservoir."

"Let's give Peter a little more time," Lucy said pleasantly.

"Amen," seconded Isobel. She was smoking furiously and drinking coffee from a container.

Timothy said nothing. He popped a Life Savers candy into his mouth and got one of his faraway extraterrestrial looks.

"Why should he show up?" an irate John Wu continued. "His bride was murdered yesterday right in front of his eyes. He's in mourning. He shouldn't go birding this morning. And you, Lucy, shouldn't have suggested it to him. Let Peter mourn in solitude and peace."

Ever so sweetly, Lucy replied, slipping almost imperceptibly into her Southern twang, "As my Aunt Hattie always says, a shotgun burying is as bad as a shotgun marrying."

John Wu, I suspected, had no idea what Aunt Hattie meant. But Lucy continued, "He wants to be with us, John. He told me so in the hospital. He's too broken up to mourn in a formal sense. He just needs friends around now. The ashes and sackcloth can wait."

"Okay, Lucy," John conceded.

We didn't have to wait much longer. Within two minutes Timothy spotted Peter Marin in his Li'l Abner finery. He was half a block away, gamely limping toward us.

"Why's he walking that way?" Isobel asked.

No one could explain it. But when Peter reached us, except for the limp and the rings under his eyes, he seemed fine. He apologized for his lateness, as Timothy had. Bird-watchers are punctual, if nothing else.

Olmsted's Irregulars marched off to the wars—Lucy Wayles on point as always, John Wu and Peter following, then Isobel, then Timothy and me.

Lucy led us up the slope behind the statute to the narrow cinder path that circled the Central Park Reservoir. Staying to the far left of the path and moving clockwise against the stream of counterclockwise joggers, we headed toward the southwest edge of the reservoir where the uncommon double-crested cormorant had been sighted, according to Wu.

"I like cormorants," Timothy said to me benignly.

"I never met one," I replied.

"They are a genetic anomaly," he said.

"I was not aware of that, Timothy," I admitted.

"Oh, yes. Unlike other waterbirds, they are unable to secrete the oil necessary to make their feathers waterproof."

All I could say was "hmm," grasping my old U.S. Navy surplus binoculars with both hands as I huffed on.

Timothy continued, "So, to get their wings dry they have to sit on a rock in the sun and stretch their wings out. They look like vampire bats from Mars."

This Timothy is a strange young man, I thought. Knowledgeable, polite, diligent, occasionally funny—but either one battery short or one too many to make the clock run on time.

Suddenly Isobel stopped short. I slammed into her. Timothy danced clear. I saw what had caused the pileup. There was an altercation in progress between John Wu and Peter Marin. They were yelling at each other.

"Gentlemen! Please!" Lucy stepped between them. "This is no time for fighting!"

"He keeps asking me the time, Lucy," John explained. "I give it to him and ten seconds later he asks for the time again. He's driving me crazy."

I found it odd that only seconds before I was using a clock metaphor to describe Timothy's strangeness to myself.

"Is this true, Peter?" Lucy asked with concern.

What happened next I shall always remember with even more intensity than the memory of that roller-blading killer of Teresa Aguilar.

Peter Marin looked at Lucy blankly, then at each and every one of us in succession. Then he bolted—running across the cinder track toward the high chain-link reservoir fence and knocking two joggers over as he went.

He climbed high up on the fence, moving incredibly swiftly for a large middle-aged man.

As he hung there, his fingers like clamps on the links of the fence, he began to sing the old spiritual "Free at Last."

Perhaps "bellow" would be a better word than "sing."

It took us forty horrendous minutes to pry his fingers loose from the fence and pull him down.

Then we half carried, half dragged the poor man to Fifth Avenue, wrestled him into a cab, and delivered him to the psychiatric intake unit of the Payne-Whitney Hospital.

Chapter 4

The admissions procedure was long and arduous—three hours worth of interviewing and filling out forms. John Wu and Isobel were the main players with Lucy for support.

By eleven-thirty in the morning poor Peter Marin had been admitted, sedated, and roomed.

Then the members of Olmsted's Irregulars scattered. I offered to drop Lucy in a cab at her apartment.

"I would prefer to walk," she said.

Payne-Whitney was on York Avenue around Sixty-eighth Street. Lucy lived on Ninety-third Street between Madison and Fifth Avenues, closer to Fifth. "But it's almost forty blocks," I remonstrated.

"I am aware of the distance," she said starchily.

I sighed and fell into step beside her. Lucy was silent. I tried to make conversation. I talked about how strange it was that Peter Marin would sing an old Negro spiritual, "Free at Last," as he was cracking up. Then I explained my theory as to why he would do such a thing: as a young man Peter no doubt heard and was moved by Martin Luther King's great speech in which he quoted the lyrics of that spiritual to make his point.

She listened politely, then patted my arm in that way of hers.

The day was growing more humid and dark. A summer storm was brewing.

When we finally turned into Ninety-third Street she asked, "Did you enjoy the walk?"

"I guess so."

"Are you fatigued?"

"Not really."

"Good. You'll need to be sharp. Because we have visitors."

I looked at her questioningly. Visitors? I saw no one.

"The car, Markus. Observe the car."

She was right. Of course. The street was empty. But there was a strange-looking vehicle double parked in front of the rather déclassé white stone building in which Lucy Wayles had a small second-floor apartment with four large windows looking out onto the street.

When we were twenty feet from the dwelling, both detectives stepped out of the unmarked vehicle.

Detective Halkin, who was wearing a blue suit that must have been terribly uncomfortable in the heat, said, "We're looking for Peter Marin."

He stared at me for a moment with what could be characterized as distaste. Why? I didn't know.

He continued, focusing on Lucy, "A neighbor of his saw him leave the house early this morning with his binoculars."

Lucy replied quickly, "Peter Marin suffered a nervous breakdown this morning in Central Park. As we were proceeding to verify a double-crested cormorant sighting. He—Peter, that is—is now in Payne-Whitney."

The detectives exchanged perplexed glances. Rupp was dressed very informally—Hunter College T-shirt, khaki pants. His weapon was clearly visible in a belt holster.

It was Rupp who edged around the car and said, "Maybe you could help us with something."

"I will do my best," Lucy promised. I nodded in affirmation.

"The tip line was buzzing last night after the TV news. One caller said that the girl Aguilar was a member of Alpha 66—a Cuban émigré terrorist organization based in Miami. Can you confirm that?"

"I didn't know Teresa Aguilar," Lucy said. "The first and last time I met her was at the wedding. But, knowing Peter, I find that implausible."

Rupp turned his thick face to me, with his eyes requesting some response from me.

"I agree," I said. "It does not seem plausible."

An angry Halkin interceded. "I'm getting so tired of you people. Nothing seems goddamn 'plausible' to you."

"I beg your pardon," Lucy snapped.

"Forget about my pardon, lady. Get observant. Start thinking. Seven bird-watchers at a bloody murder. And no one can tell us anything."

I could see Lucy beginning to get angry . . .

like a copperhead testing her rattles. Softly, lethally, she responded.

"Your arithmetic, Detective, is a bit faulty. There were only six bird-watchers at the wedding. But I do realize that excellence in addition and subtraction is not a criteria for promotion in the police department."

Uh-oh, I thought. This is going to get nasty.

Detective Halkin unbuttoned his suit jacket and threw up his hands. "Bird-watchers. Girl watchers. *Whale* watchers! Whatever. Seven people saw that killing!"

Lucy smiled. "Perhaps it's the heat. Or the humidity. New York in August is always difficult. Even, I suppose, for a native son like yourself. But . . . ah . . . how shall I put it . . . . . . *eight* people saw the murder. Six bird-watchers, the minister, and the boy. Ten, if you count the murderer and his victim."

Almost as if they had rehearsed it, both detectives shouted in desperate unison: "What boy?"

"Tell them, Markus," Lucy ordered casually.

I hadn't the slightest idea what she was talking about.

She clucked at my stupidity. Then she said, "The minister and the bride came down the slope, accompanied by a young man carrying a folding table and champagne."

Oh. Oh, yes, of course. I remembered then.

But the boy had not been around after the murder. He had vanished completely—from the crime scene and from my mind as well. In the heat and the horror and the blood, and mesmerized by that roller-blading angel of death, he had become invisible.

A grim Detective Rupp asked Lucy, "May I use your phone?"

"Of course."

We all went up to the apartment.

Hell-bent on proving that Lucy's eighth man theory was ridiculous, the detectives seemed oblivious to the peculiar charms of her domicile. May I enumerate them?

First and foremost—a dazzling display of bird prints on the walls—in styles ranging from the realistic to the surreal.

Second—huge piles of books, journals, magazines, and clippings on the floor, turning the living room into a modest mountain range.

Third—a cat named Dipper who hung about high on top of doors, cabinets, and bookcases, hissing and spitting like a cornered mountain lion.

But Detectives Rupp and Halkin ignored their surroundings. Halkin dialed the number of William Aaron, the Unitarian minister who had officiated at the aborted wedding ceremony.

There was obviously some animated discourse going on but I could not make out the words.

Then Halkin hung up and announced, "Reverend Aaron says the young man just showed up as he was escorting the bride through the park. He assumed Marin had hired him but never inquired further. And he doesn't know when or why the boy vanished."

"Would you like some iced tea?" Lucy inquired.

No. They wanted nothing. They were an impatient, unhappy pair. Flipping out their notebooks, they questioned Lucy and me about the boy. They particularly wanted a physical description.

All Lucy could give them was that the eighth man was of slight build and about twenty years old.

I recalled that his hair was dark, curly, and

closely shorn, and he wore cutoff jeans and sneakers.

The detectives left as swiftly as they had entered. Lucy then made the iced tea. I waited, happy to be in her apartment. Of course I was a little fearful; after all, Dipper longed to leap down on me and rip my beating heart out.

When she handed me the tall glass, I said, "Lucy, I have some questions to ask you."

"About what?"

"Laughing gulls."

"What a strange topic to be concerning yourself with now, Markus."

"But look. You told me to beware the laughing gull. And I am. I'm trying to. But really, I can't understand what a gull that laughs because it can't sing has to do with a thuggish three-legged pit bull or with the murder of Peter's bride. At least, in the case of the white-eared hummingbird, and the leks, I had an inkling of some connection. Lucy, you are confusing me—again."

She patted me on the head and sat down. She looked beautiful without the headband too. Lucy had a new haircut—a sort of Joan of Arc style. Her hair is almost all white now but she looks younger to me. Is that love, when the object of one's affections seems constantly to grow younger?

She sat as she always did: the very definition of erect, ramrod-straight, hands folded primly on her lap.

"I have a question for *you*, Markus."

"Yes?"

"Did those two detectives remind you of something?"

"No."

"Ah well, to me they quite resemble two downy woodpeckers trying to build a nest in an aluminum flagpole, mistaking it for a maple. Am I straying too far from the mark?"

"I think not," I replied, not knowing enough about downy woodpeckers to make a truly seasoned judgment.

"Thank you. Now for a more important question."

"Shoot."

"Did it ever occur to you, Markus, that there is a traitor in the ranks of Olmsted's Irregulars?"

"Never!" I asserted vigorously.

"Are you sure?"

"Well, fairly sure."

"You are a trusting man," she countered, her voice just a bit patronizing around the edges.

"Listen, Lucy, I don't understand the question. We started this conversation with laughing gulls. Now we're on to traitors. But a traitor to what? To whom? And for goodness' sake, why?"

She was silent. I, on the other hand, was getting pretty worked up.

"Do you mean a traitor to downy woodpeckers?" I asked.

"Oh, Markus. You do have a poetic streak, don't you? Alas, I must attend to my laundry now. My best to Duke."

I should have known something was coming. I really should have. But I didn't. I merely showed up whistling "Dixie," thinking this would be just another delicious avian trek under the tutelage of my true love, just like all the others—except, of course, our colleague Peter Marin would be absent.

So I was as surprised as the others when Lucy announced to the troops gathered in front of the statue at 7 A.M.: "Today, since a morning lightning storm is predicted, there will be no expedition. I shall instead buy you all the most delicious of breakfasts."

I had no knowledge of any impending storm—lightning or otherwise. I had been listening to the radio before leaving my apartment. Surely there would have been some report on the storm.

"Do you mean now?" Isobel asked Lucy.

"Right now," she said. "Follow me."

And, like always, we did. She led us into a magnificent new Belgian café on Madison Avenue just south of Eighty-sixth Street. The sudden appearance of a flock of bird-watchers did not disturb the staff in the least. Indeed, considering the speed with which they seated us at the large butcher block table and delivered a huge tray of sweet rolls, muffins, tarts, and croissants, they must have been expecting our visit. Lucy, I decided, had set this gathering up in advance of her announcement in the park. She had probably arranged for it the night before.

I was seated next to young Timothy, who kept on adjusting his eyeglass frames on his nose and staring oddly at the pile of pastries. It occurred to me that he might well be a secret health food enthusiast. After all, science fiction writers tend to be a bit weird. But then, in one incredibly swift motion of his gangly arm, he plucked a cherry tart from the pile and bit into it with fastidious ferocity.

Something else dawned on me: that Timothy, being an African-American, would appreciate what I thought was my rather brilliant analysis of Peter Marin's behavior the other day. Remember, Peter had bellowed out "Free at last!" during his nervous breakdown. At least Timothy would appreciate it more than Lucy had.

Then we made our selections from the impressive coffee menu—espresso, cappuccino, European concoctions with floating whipped cream, decaf variations on all the choices.

I ordered a cup of American coffee. Everyone else ordered some kind of coffee except Timothy, who ordered orange pekoe tea with honey.

We breakfasted hugely and for the most part in silence.

After a while Lucy tapped softly on the table with her spoon. John Wu smiled. Isobel gave out a little guffaw. *Aha!* everyone was thinking, the ulterior motive is now about to be revealed. Let's face facts . . . this whole breakfast was suspicious.

"I thought you'd all want to know that I was

in touch with the hospital early this morning. Peter will be released shortly. He seems to have recovered his equilibrium. And it appears he is threatening the hospital with a lawsuit on the grounds he was admitted under a fraudulent diagnosis. Anyway, he'll probably be out tomorrow."

There was scattered applause in response to Lucy's announcement.

Isobel whispered to me, "He probably contacted that advocacy group that represents hospitalized mental patients. They fight to get you out." Then she forked a muffin.

Lucy proceeded to describe to the others our conversation with the detectives concerning the mystery boy who carried the folding table and champagne.

"If you have any further information concerning him," she counseled, "please contact Detectives Rupp and Halkin."

This raised a veritable storm of confused memories. They all now remembered him. But they all, like Lucy and I, had lost sight of him in the chaos after the shooting.

John Wu said, "I don't believe he was hired by Peter. Remember? He said there would be food and drink *after* the ceremony—at his apartment. But Peter probably thought the minister had provided the table and champagne. All signals were crossed."

Isobel said, "I think he was an accomplice in the murder. At least, that's what I think now."

"He looked like one of the Beastie Boys," noted Timothy.

But before anyone could question Timothy as to just what or who a Beastie Boy was Lucy began speaking again, in a very peculiar tone. I do mean peculiar.

She said quietly, wistfully, with a faraway look in her eye: "I want to share a very personal reminiscence. Many years ago when I was a librarian at the University of North Carolina in Chapel Hill, I fell in love with a pharmacist named Buford."

I sat back, stunned, as if someone had given me a sudden whack on the head. I thought I knew about all of Lucy's lovers from the past. There weren't many. But she had never mentioned a Buford. Were there a lot more she hadn't told me about? Why had she hidden him from me? Had I become too ardent a suitor? Was she afraid to tell me the truth about her past because she feared I would become unstable and violent? All my jealousy stemmed from the simple fact that my love for her was still unrequited.

Isobel Soba cast me a compassionate glance. And I think I felt Timothy's knee against mine for just a moment under the table. Male solidarity transcends generational gaps, you know.

Lucy continued, "We had many an argument because I was even then a passionate bird-watcher—and he was a passionate hunter of waterfowl. His greatest joy in life was to be in a blind in the marsh, just before dawn, with his shotgun, his dog, his decoys, his duck calls, and his fellow hunters.

"Buford always used to say that he loved me dearly but nothing provided him with such intensive camaraderie as those early mornings in the marsh waiting to shoot ducks and geese. Eventually I could not tolerate his hunting passion even though I knew that hunters are the most fervent supporters of wildlife preservation policies. It is a sad contradiction.

"But believe me, I knew what he was talking about. Intense camaraderie? Yes. Those were Buford's exact words. And I have always experienced that among bird-watchers."

She looked—nay, glared—about the table in a sudden shift of mood.

"And isn't that what the Olmsted's Irregulars are all about?" she asked.

There were impassioned nods all around the table.

"So, you can image my horror when I realized that this most precious bond between us had been savaged by one of our members. Particularly since we are in dark times."

One by one, we all commenced to squirm. I remembered her comments about a traitor among us. But who was she really talking about? And how had this individual broken the bond of camaraderie?

The she smiled sweetly, sadly, pointed at John Wu, and asked, "Is this not the case?"

Elegant Mr. Wu (he always wore tennis garb for bird-watching treks) looked positively shocked. Then his eyes narrowed.

"Please explain yourself," he said curtly.

"Oh, I shall! On the morning of Peter Marin's collapse you recounted to us the events which occurred just prior to his breakdown. Peter kept asking you for the time. You gave it to him. Then he asked again. And again you told him. You gave it to him. Then he asked again. And again you told him. On and on until there was an altercation. Is this not so, John?"

"Yes, that is what happened."

"But, the John Wu I know would have handled it differently. He would have, after the second loony request for the time, simply handed his watch to Peter. That you did not act according to your usual style, John, means that something else was going on with Peter, or between you and Peter. I do believe that. My guess is that there was some kind of secret pact in place. As Aunt Hattie once said: If the preacher and the banjo player are seeing the same gal, the hymns get weird."

There was silence. Sometimes Lucy (and for that matter her Aunt Hattie, who had, thankfully, visited New York only once) was so brilliant that she left everyone in the dust.

John Wu fiddled with his coffee spoon.

Lucy said gently to him, "Confide in us, dear. We surely need that camaraderie. These are dark times indeed."

He quietly placed the spoon beside his saucer, and confessed.

"I went to see Peter after he announced he was

going to be married in the park. I went at night and I went alone. You all know how impulsive he is in affairs of the heart. I wanted to caution him against rushing into this marriage."

He halted there. But Lucy kept after him. "And what happened?"

"Well, he thought you had sent me. I assured him I came of my own volition and that whatever he said to me would be held in strictest confidence. He wouldn't listen to reason, though. He said he loved this woman more than life itself; that she was the most wonderful woman he had ever met; that he was blissfully happy—blissful, period."

"*Bliss*ful?" questioned Isobel, her voice like the blare of a trumpet.

"Yes. That was his word. He said he appreciated my concern but there was no cause for it."

"And what did he tell you about Teresa Aguilar?" Lucy asked.

"Not much," admitted John. "That she was thirty-one years old. Born in Cuba. Raised in Tampa. Moved to New York a few years ago. Alone in the world. Small apartment in Sunnyside, Queens. She made dresses for a living, selling them wherever she could. They were 'wonderful Caribbean garments,' Peter said."

Lucy pressed on. "Is that all?"

John thought for a minute. "Also that she loved birds. He said she had a passion for birds."

"Did he tell you how and where he met her?"

"No."

"And then what happened?" she said.

"Nothing. We had a few drinks and I left."

There was a long silence.

Finally Lucy said, "I want to thank you for sharing that information with us. Sometimes, confidences must be broken."

John looked most unhappy.

Timothy piped up: "I like that phrase 'dark times.'"

Isobel went out for a smoke then.

I began to brood about Buford.

We never went birding that morning. We picked the pastry tray clean and studied the walls of the café on which were hung photos of the bucolic Belgian countryside.

I returned home early in the afternoon. The minute I entered the apartment I knew that something was wrong.

I heard chewing sounds.

Was he at my shoes again? I strode into his bedroom to confront him. But Duke wasn't there. Then I realized that the sounds were coming from the kitchen.

He wasn't chewing my shoes on the kitchen floor, nor any other object from my wardrobe. He was chewing himself—biting and licking the top of his left front paw.

And the area he was attacking was already raw.

I sat down on the kitchen chair. "You'd better leave that paw alone," I warned him.

He ignored me, as usual, and kept right on chomping. Whatever had happened to his paw since the morning, his ministrations were making it worse.

And so it had come to this. I was going to have to treat the beast.

It occurred to me that a retired physician such as myself (even though I was a researcher rather than a practitioner) should have a basic first aid kit on the premises.

Alas, all I had on hand was a bottle of hydrogen peroxide, some ancient cotton balls, and a roll of very old gauze. Well, that would have to do.

I collected all the implements of mercy from the bathroom cabinet and returned to my three-legged patient.

He gave me a startled look as I knelt down beside him.

"All I'm going to do is clean that paw up a bit and bandage it," I assured Duke, using my prettiest bedside manner and hoping it would inspire confidence in the patient.

Pit bulls have beady eyes—no insult intended—it's simply a fact. And Duke kept his on me as I opened the bottle of peroxide and proceeded to use it to a wet a cotton ball.

When I moved the cotton toward the paw, I heard a very distinct sound—quite resonant—a rumbling that seemed to come from the pit of his stomach.

I stopped the forward movement of my arm so quickly that I fell over backward.

I recovered and, as usual, tried to reason with him. "Now, Duke, I understand fully that we are not the best of friends. In fact, the condition that exists between us could even be described as one consisting chiefly of mutual dislike—even loathing—and certainly fear plays its part in the relationship. But I assure you, what I am doing now is in your best interests. Help often comes from people you don't like. That is the way it is in the world, Duke."

Once again I slowly pushed the cotton ball toward the inflamed area.

This time, Duke dropped his head onto the floor, laid his ears all the way back, and gave me a sly, sickening smile—the pit bull way of signaling that an attack was imminent.

I got out of there on the double, leaving the treatment paraphernalia on the floor, all of it: bottle, cotton, and gauze.

Sitting in my living-room armchair, I pondered the situation. I could hear him chewing on his paw. The only rational thing to do was take him for a walk and lead him, unsuspecting, into a veterinarian's office.

I looked at the clock. Gregor, the doorman, would still be on duty. He was a kindly, plump West Indian who had no fewer than three rottweilers. Surely Gregor would know a good vet in the neighborhood.

Of course I could consult Lucy. But no, at this point Gregor was probably the better bet.

I snoozed a bit in the chair, taking a kind of weary forty winks, like a combat surgeon resting up before the bloody battle. Then I got to my feet, grabbed Duke's leash off the doorknob, and shook it to get the beast's attention.

Duke, who loved to be walked, even by me, came hopping over.

I locked the door behind us. Off we went. It was going to be a long walk, I soon realized. Out in the hallway, he hopped for three or four steps, then plopped down to perform his chewing ritual, then began hopping again.

When we reached the lobby, Gregor immediately perceived the situation. He ambled over in his peculiar costume. Gregor always wore a spiffy doorman's coat and hat with copious gold braiding, but then, as if to declare his independence from the powers that be, he completed the outfit with decidedly unconventional trousers—work pants, in fact, with old paint smudges all over them. Actually, from the first moment he appeared I found the mix appealing. After all, I too suffer from the disorder known as, perhaps, garment confusion. Someone in the birding group—very likely John Wu—had once described me as sartorially challenged. My troubles in this regard have no doubt hurt the progress of my pursuit of Lucy Wayles.

"Trouble, Doc, huh?" the amiable Gregor said.

"Yes. Trouble."

He stood over the three-legged Duke.

"He seemed fine this morning," Gregor noted.

"True. But when I got back a little while ago, he was chewing on that front paw like a madman."

"Umm, I hate those hot spots."

"Are you sure it's one of those?" I asked.

"Doc, believe me, when it comes to this area you are looking at a diagnostic genius."

"I don't doubt it, Gregor. But listen, do you know of a reliable vet in the neighborhood?"

"Forget a vet."

"Why?"

"The only thing they do is give you one of those collars so the dog can't get to the thing he's trying to chew. But you really don't want to put one of those Queen Elizabeth restraining collars on this dog, Doc. I mean, look at him. He's got enough trouble."

"You have a point. But I think a qualified vet should check him out."

"No one knows what the hell they are, Doc.

Not even the vets. When you're talking hot spots, you're talking mystery. Some people say bacteria. Some say virus. Some say allergy. No one knows. You understand what I'm saying?"

"Well, Gregor, until they do a valid epidemiological study, I had better stick with conventional science. Isn't there a vet on Fifty-fifth Street near Ninth?"

He appeared not to be listening to me at all. "Zeus had one about a year ago."

"What? Who is Zeus?"

"One of my rotties. Oh, he was hurting."

"And?"

"I cured him."

"How?"

He gestured that I should follow him to the desk. When I complied, he sat down and said in an almost conspiratorial whisper, "Bitter Apple."

"What is that?"

"It takes care of those hot spots."

"How is it administered?"

"What do you mean, Doc?"

"What I mean is, do you give it to them orally? An IV? What?"

"No, no. It's a liquid. You know."

"How do you apply it?"

"Just dump it on."

"And how does it work?"

"Well, Doc, it's sort of a deterrent. The stuff tastes so bad, the doggie just won't go back to the wound."

"Is it safe?"

"As safe as Jack Daniel's."

"And what does that mean?" I asked, growing alarmed.

"It's made of fermented apples," he explained. "Sure it's safe. And it's got some other ingredients. Rubbing alcohol. Bittering agents. Some things that cauterize the sore. A few goodies like that. Oh, it's a honey."

"And you're sure it works?"

"It works. Ask Zeus."

I hesitated. It wasn't that I didn't trust Gregor; I did. But . . .

"Now listen to me, Doc. I'm going to tell you the whole story—straight. Look at Duke. You call that a hot spot? It's nothing to what my Zeus had. I mean, he was digging chunks of flesh out of his groin. And it had happened sudden . . . oh, so sudden . . . he just started chewing. So I figured just like you figured: take him to a vet. Especially after he almost rearranged my face when

I tried to look at the wound. Need I say this made me very nervous. I got three rotties . . . but Zeus is the only male and he's the sweetest and gentlest of the three. But now he like to take off one side of my face just because I'm interfering with his chewing. Oh, yeah, it was time to move. So, like I said, I take him to the vet."

Gregor paused here and began to breathe raggedly, as if the mere recounting of this story and the accompanying painful memories were causing him great distress.

"So?" I pushed him to go on.

"So I took him. I don't even want to go into all the nonsense that went on. I mean a whole lot of nonsense. Yeah, they tried the collar. And you know what Zeus did? He's smart. He hooked it on to one of the spokes from the fence and just ripped it away. Then they gave him antibiotics, and all kind of tranquilizers and muscle relaxers, but meanwhile, all the time Zeus kept eating away at that spot and it was getting real serious."

He sat up straight suddenly, took off his hat, blew into it, and replaced it. "That's the story."

"And what happened then?"

"I heard about this Bitter Apple. I used it. And that was that."

I was still a bit skeptical, but then I thought about Duke readying himself to attack me. I thought about Gregor's dog nearly ripping off his face. "Where do I get it?"

"There's a place on Forty-fourth Street near Eighth Avenue. A pet store. They sell birds, fish, geckoes . . . and Bitter Apple."

"Do geckoes get hot spots?" I was trying to make a joke.

"I believe," Gregor said thoughtfully, "that all creatures of the earth get a variant of them, including Homo sapiens."

"That's a long walk for Duke in his condition. Surely there's a pet store closer than that."

"Now listen to me, Doc. I have to explain myself better, I guess. This Bitter Apple is fine stuff. But it ain't made by a corporation. You get me?"

"I do. I understand now."

"It's made by an old lady in Connecticut. She brews it up herself, bottles it herself, and ships it herself. Only a few places carry it."

"So we're talking about a home remedy here, Gregor?" I asked.

"What we're talking about, Doc, is Bitter Apple," he replied cryptically.

I thought it over.

The upside was, it might work. And Gregor was right about it being very cruel to put one of those funnel-shaped restricting collars on Duke, even if he was, as Lucy's Aunt Hattie said, "a no-account pit bull."

The downside? I couldn't even get to Duke's paw with a cotton ball. How was I going to treat the hot spot with this apple concoction? And what if the stuff was just plain old voodoo science?

Gregor saw me twisting in the winds of contradiction and he had compassion.

"Listen," he said, "let me help you out here. You go get it. I'll walk Duke. Me and him get along fine."

This was what swayed me, finally. After all, walking Duke was no picnic, for a variety of reasons, among them—

1) Basic animosity . . . primal fear . . . eternal distrust between this man and this dog.

2) People sympathetic with his plight as a three-legged pooch always tried to engage one or both of us in conversation. Some tried to pet him.

Some tried to lecture me, as if I were responsible for his plight. Some gave me their views about the minds and souls of pit bulls and why they were considered so dangerous. Several times in the past I've had individuals press money into my hands and urge me to start a fund in order to get him a prosthetic device. And one woman had attacked me physically because it was obvious to her that I had willfully malnourished him.

3) Picking up after Duke usually sent my back into spasm.

So the die was cast. I walked alone, briskly, to the pet store.

The small woman behind the counter was wearing those gypsy earrings. I found her alluring. She was not, however, the friendliest merchant I had ever run across.

And the store was a bit dank and untidy. The chattering of creatures could be heard even from outside. I immediately spotted several tanks of geckoes and other lizards. The tanks were spotlessly clean and illuminated.

"Yes?"

For some reason I asked her, "Who buys geckoes?"

"People."

"Oh?"

"People buy geckoes. Who did you think bought them? Frogs and bunny rabbits don't come in here and buy them."

"Yes, I understand that. I mean, *why* do people buy them."

"Companionship—or roaches. The geckoes eat cockroaches. And they often stay in the same place without moving for long periods of time. Lonely people find that very soothing."

This woman, I decided, had an odd view of life. One of her earrings seemed to move. I wondered why Lucy never wore jewelry like this. She did wear earrings on occasion, but small ones that never dangled, always nestling right against her earlobe. I wondered if I should purchase a pair of gold hoops for her. Would she be pleased or insulted?

"Can I help you with something?"

"Oh, sorry—yes, yes," I said, coming out of my reverie. "I would like a bottle of Bitter Apple."

Then I added, "My dog has a hot spot on his paw."

"Bitter Apple doesn't come in 'bottles.' It

comes in a plastic squeeze dispenser. Like ketchup at a roadside diner."

The image was not an especially pleasant one, but, as I said, the die was cast.

"Whatever it comes in, I'll take it."

"Small, medium, or large?"

"Small."

She gave me a disapproving look, as if I were conserving money at the expense of my dog's health. But she vanished and returned with the object, which she placed delicately on the counter.

I picked it up and began to study the label.

"Is there a problem?" she asked.

"No. I'm just curious about the ingredients."

"Bitter Apple is bitter apple," she said caustically and then added, "That will be thirteen ninety-nine with the tax."

A bit steep, I thought, for such a small bottle of such an unknown and unproven substance. In fact, the hastily handwritten label inspired even less confidence in the contents.

I paid for it anyway, and promptly returned to my apartment building, where Duke, apparently happy with his stroll, was now tethered to a lobby chair, calmly chewing away at his paw.

"Good luck," called Gregor as the dog and I entered the elevator.

The moment we got back inside, I poured out some choice dog food into Duke's dish, even though it wasn't yet feeding time. I hoped that would distract him from his paw long enough for me to safely apply the medication.

Alas, Duke totally ignored the food and plopped down on the kitchen floor to worry his paw.

I thought of my shoes. I rushed into the bedroom and brought back my choice dress shoes, the ones Duke had already ravaged. He paid them no mind at all.

I sat down on a kitchen chair and attempted to formulate a strategy. Perhaps I'd better call Lucy after all, I thought. She had no fear of the beast. In fact, according to her, Duke was a "pussycat," and in fact, he acted like one when she was around. When it was just Duke and me, though, he gave out strong hints that he was a mountain lion crossed with a dingo.

No, I wouldn't call Lucy. She'd only make fun of me. It would be just another in an endless line of blows to our courtship. After all, I was doing all kinds of things to make her believe that I was brave, creative, gentle, strong. Wasn't I bird-watching up a storm now? And dressing more carefully. And trying to learn how to cook.

I sat up straight in my chair. Chicken livers and mushrooms. Yes, that was the dish I was experimenting with because the recipe had appeared so simple: just throw the chicken livers into the pan, then the mushrooms, then the spices.

And, as a matter of fact, I had some raw chicken livers left . . . bloody, smelly, tiny little ones.

How could any dog—even a pit bull—withstand them?

I rushed to the refrigerator and brought the container back to the table. I opened the lid and peered inside. Three left. Little beauties of raw and rare enticement.

I stared at Duke. Why delay? It was now or never.

I picked up the Bitter Apple with my left hand, flipped open the cap, and gave a little squeeze to make sure it was squirting properly. I sniffed the product. My, it was powerful, whatever was in there.

I planned my next move with great care. It

would be best, I realized, to meet Duke on his own terrain. That is, on all fours, down on the kitchen floor. I would dangle one of the chicken livers and entice him away from his preoccupation with his paw.

As the seduction was proceeding, I would squirt the sore limb with the Bitter Apple, the squeeze container being kept hidden from him while the enticement was taking place.

My plan was brilliant in its simplicity. Given all the current turmoil in my life—what with the murder and such—it amazed me that I had come up with such an elegant therapeutic intervention.

Still, I hesitated.

Perhaps it was the chicken livers that made me do so. My efforts with them so far had been poor. No doubt about that. My gourmet dish had come out of the sauté pan looking like hell and tasting like—how can I put it politely?—like slop. I was sure that the ancillary ingredients, the spices for instance, had been my downfall.

Duke went on chewing.

"You are behaving like a fool," I said to him.

He raised his eyes a bit and squinted at me. I'd looked into those eyes a thousand times, and they still gave me the shivers.

I closed my own eyes then. No more stalling. It was time to act. I had to buttress my courage. Now, what was that poem we had had to memorize in fifth grade? Oh, yes, something about the boy standing on a burning deck.

But I couldn't get past the first line.

I leapt into the fray—a raw morsel in my right hand, Bitter Apple in my left, neatly concealed.

On all fours, believe me, I felt my age. This was a young man's game.

Duke was still lacerating his injured paw.

Suddenly, like a mongoose hypnotizing a snake, I bobbed and weaved, waving the liver in front of his nose. At last the cur noticed me and the delectable I was wagging in front of him. His eyes went stupid with desire.

I moved the meat, wiggled it, pushed it closer to his nose, and then pulled it away.

He groaned loudly, elevated himself, and lunged.

Quickly, with great precision, like a matador now, I squirted the Bitter Apple onto his paw, saturating it.

Duke yelped, abandoning the liver.

But the pain of the application lasted only a

moment and then he just looked dumbly down at his paw.

I got up and returned to my chair—waiting, watching.

No sooner had I sat down than he returned his attention to the paw. He licked it only once, and then yanked his head away, going into a paroxysm of blinking and spitting. He recovered, tried again—and again and again—each time pulling away quickly and starting the spit-blink-and-groan routine anew.

At last, he rose and hobbled from one side of the kitchen to the other. He would stop and stare uncomprehendingly at the paw. Obviously he wanted to chew it again, but just as obviously, he wanted no part of that taste again.

Duke walked over to his feed bowl, ate some, and then hopped into his bedroom, to rest and reflect, I presumed.

I repaired to the living-room chair, my knees aching, but glorying in my triumph over that dumb beast.

Yes, Gregor had been right. Bitter Apple had done the job, with no loss of life or limb and only minimal pain and discomfort.

But that is what the practice of medicine is all

about: a little pain, a little discomfort for the greater good.

I reached into the bottom shelf of the small table next to my chair, retrieved a cut-glass decanter, and poured myself two fingers of Martel Cordon Bleu cognac. The moment the first sip went down, several rather perplexing thoughts came to me . . . no, not about Duke and his paw. The first one was about the dreadful murder in the park.

The second thought concerned my colleagues John Wu and Peter Marin.

I began to think also about Lucy's performance in the coffee shop, where she had wormed out of John the confession that he, in light of his special relationship with Peter, had tried to dissuade Peter from marrying.

Why those thoughts had surfaced just then no doubt had to do with my crawling around the kitchen on all fours, holding the raw, reeking liver in my hand. Unusual behavior can often unlock the floodgates of the unconscious.

I took another long sip of that very expensive brandy and it burned brightly as it went down.

What if . . . what if John had tried to do for Peter Marin what I had done for Duke? A little therapeutic pain for a worthy cause, for a greater good.

What if John Wu, out of affection for Peter, had hired someone to disrupt the ceremony in order to save Peter from a doomed marriage?

What if the killing had simply been an accident? The man John hired had lost control of the situation and fired into the bride rather than into the air. What if there wasn't supposed to be a murder at all—merely a disruption?

I set the brandy glass aside. This was, I realized, the wildest kind of speculation. Too wild even for a member of Olmsted's Irregulars. But I did know something that the other Irregulars did not. I mean, as a birder I am often pathetic. Yet, in the realm of human complexity, Markus Bloch is often dazzlingly intuitive. Would it be immodest to say brilliant?

John Wu was a fastidious, mannerly, rational gentleman who dealt with hard financial transactions. At least on the face of it that was what he was.

As in my case, however, with John there lay just beneath the surface the wild romanticism of a pirate on the Spanish main, a buccaneer—or maybe a Dadaist.

A Dadaist?

I realized my speculations had now gone off the map. I got up and tiptoed into Duke's room. He was asleep on the rug. Well, it had been a long day for him, and it wasn't over yet. I walked into the kitchen and sat down in front of that strange-looking Bitter Apple squeeze container.

It dawned on me that I should obtain the address of the old woman in Connecticut who brews up the stuff and nominate her for the Nobel Prize.

Chapter 5

When the Irregulars gathered the next morning, there was excitement in the air. And it had nothing to do with events or persons pertaining to that murderous wedding in the park.

It was a feeling . . . a rustling . . . a message on the soft wind that the southbound migration was about to begin, however slowly and tentatively.

Oh, it was a bit early, but Canada was already beginning to chill a bit, sending autumnlike breezes through New England, and some of the birds were starting for Honduras or wherever. Central Park would be their first stop.

I could sense the edginess in the others when I showed up. They were sniffing at the air and pawing the ground like colts.

As for me, I faked it. Why? Well, the first birds

to begin arriving—the vanguard, if you will—are always warblers, and I couldn't tell one from the other. I like warblers in an academic sense; nothing more.

The only warbler I feel any affinity for is the blue-winged specimen, probably because Lucy had once told me that they develop regional dialects in their songs. I have always been interested in regional dialects. In this context it meant that some blue-winged warblers sounded like Willie Nelson, some like the Beach Boys, and some like Little Richard, or maybe even Pete Seeger. At least I thought it possible.

Actually, the only time I get really excited bird-watching—forgetting that I took it up strictly as a courtship ploy—is in late September when the big boys start zooming over and in. I'm referring to the birds of prey: hawks, falcons, owls. Then you practically have to give me a sedative.

Anyway, at seven sharp, with Lucy in the lead, we headed north on the horse trail. It was a cloudy morning with a strange warm wind kicking up around us.

We hadn't walked more than fifty yards when we heard someone behind us shout: "Stop! Stop! I said *Stop!*"

Startled, we turned in unison, like a drill team.

There was Peter Marin, not ten feet away from us. And what a sight he was.

Peter was in full formal evening dress. He was wearing a tuxedo and, incongruously, carrying a paper shopping bag.

The first thought I had was that he really must have gone mad, as he was wearing the costume he should have worn for his wedding, but of course did not. Now it was too late for dressing up.

"Why?" Peter shouted in anguish, and to no one in particular. "Why did you do that to me?"

"Do what?" John responded.

"Put me in that horrible place!"

This seemed to infuriate Isobel Soba. She stomped out her cigarette and propelled her short wide body right up to Peter, poking him in the chest as she beat out her tattoo of words.

"You all-fired fool! Do you know what you were doing when we pulled you down? You had climbed up on the reservoir fence. You were crazy. You were singing. We had to fight to get your fingers loose from that fence. What did you want us to do with you? Take you to Eighty-sixth Street and buy you a papaya drink?"

The assault seemed to calm Peter. The big red-head started muttering to himself. Then he stepped past Isobel and confronted Lucy.

"When I walked out of that prison this morning, I was met—"

John Wu would not allow him to finish that sentence. "Payne-Whitney is not a prison, Peter. It's one of the finest private mental hospitals in the world!"

Marin brushed the objection aside with a beefy hand. "When I got out of penal servitude this morning, who should be there waiting for me but those two detectives. Imagine it. I simply couldn't believe their gall. First they demanded the name of the boy who came to the wedding with a folding table and champagne. Now, how the hell should I know his name? *I* didn't invite him; *I* didn't hire him. I never saw him before in my life. And then they had the audacity to ask me if Teresa had been a member of some right-wing Cuban death squad—Gamma 67 or some such nonsense."

"You mean Alpha 66," John corrected him, "and they're not a death squad, strictly speaking."

"Who cares what they are!" Peter bellowed. "Can you believe those idiot policemen?"

Lucy clucked in sympathy. Then she asked gently, "Are you coming with us into the park, Peter?"

"No! Are you coming with *me*?"

"Where do you mean, dear?"

"To the funeral," he choked out.

He pointed downward, into the shopping bag. We gathered around it and stared. Inside the bag was a large lacquered wood box.

The group members exchanged quick glances. We knew instantly what we were looking at. The box no doubt contained the ashes of Peter's bride-to-be, Teresa Aguilar.

"She wished to be buried at sea," Peter announced. "And I shall carry out that request faithfully. Since she lived in Queens and I in Manhattan, I shall release the ashes into the East River from the deck of the Circle Line ferry the moment we sail under the Queensboro Bridge. This morning."

"You can't do that, Peter," John admonished. "It's illegal. You'll be arrested. You're not allowed to throw anything into the East River from a boat or the shore."

Heedless, Peter waved away the warning. He took hold of the bag, lifted it off the ground. "Are you people coming or not?" he challenged.

No one said a word. But when Lucy linked her arm through Peter's, we followed them out of the park.

So that was how, at eight o'clock that morning, the Olmsted's Irregulars came to be seated on the lower deck of the Circle Line ferry as it headed out of its slip at Forty-second Street and the Hudson River to begin its circumnavigation of Manhattan Island.

The tourists for the most part gravitated toward the upper deck.

It was a macabre scene, but only for those who knew what was in that shopping bag. We sat together in absolute silence as the big ferry moved down the Hudson toward the bay, preparatory to swinging around the tip of Manhattan and then going north up the East River.

From time to time the tour guide's bored voice was heard over the loudspeaker, pointing out landmarks and relevant details on the passing scene for the tourists.

Timothy was the only one who seemed to be

enjoying himself; at least he was doing something. He had fixed his binoculars on the twin towers of the World Trade Center. Perhaps he was looking for high-nesting falcons. Perhaps. But I had the feeling he was on the lookout for some signs of some kind of extraterrestrial communication.

Peter sat between Lucy and me. He held himself stiffly in his tuxedo. The breeze from the water blew through his hair and beard. The shopping bag was in his lap.

When we rounded the tip of the island and entered the East River, I saw the bridges. Now, I have lived in New York all my life, but I still don't know the accurate succession of those East River bridges.

All I know is that the Queensboro Bridge—or the Fifty-ninth Street Bridge as it is more commonly known—was the fourth one.

The three before it, going upriver from south to north, were the Brooklyn, the Manhattan, and the Williamsburg.

Snatches of the very strange conversation taking place between Peter Marin and Lucy interrupted my focus on New York trivia.

"How do you feel, Peter? I mean, really."

"Excellent, Lucy."

"The river does refresh, doesn't it?"

"So it does."

"She was a lovely young woman, Peter. She had a simple beauty that one rarely sees anymore."

"She was that, and more."

"Where did you meet?"

For the longest time he did not answer. His eyes had filled with tears and he kept moving his head from side to side. I saw Lucy place one of her hands on his.

Finally he regained control and was able to speak again. "I met her in a distant land. Far away. It was a place so strange and filled with such beauty and virtue that the vultures were allergic to carrion. Can you imagine a land like that, Lucy?"

She began her reply to his bizarre statements, but then stopped herself.

No more words were exchanged between them.

I closed my eyes and dozed for a bit. After all, it had been years since my last sea journey.

When I opened them we were fast approaching the designated bridge. For some reason I whispered to myself, "The bridge at Remagen." Then I realized that was the title of a 1960s movie about World War Two.

Peter stood up abruptly, straightened his cummerbund, and walked swiftly, purposefully, to the rail.

We all followed on his heels and surrounded him, attempting to shield his criminal act from the eyes of our fellow passengers and the crew.

Peter removed the box from its carrier.

"John," he said, "the words, please."

A startled and perplexed John Wu replied in a hoarse whisper, "What words? What are you talking about?"

"The ceremony for Christian burial at sea," replied Peter.

"How should I know that!"

"You were an officer in the U.S. Navy in your youth, John."

"Yes, but so what? Your head's in another century, man! They haven't buried people at sea for a long, long time. They put them in body bags and keep them refrigerated until the ship docks."

Peter shook his head mournfully. We were by then directly beneath the Queensboro.

He opened the lacquered box and dumped the

ashes without another word. Then he flung the box into the water. Finally he ripped the shopping bag into shreds and tossed those overboard as well.

We all stood right there at the rail for the remainder of the long trip around Manhattan.

The moment we docked, Peter ripped off his tie and cummerbund. "Do you have any cash on you?" he asked John.

"Yes."

"Good. We must have a wake."

Peter then led us several blocks north and into a god-awful waterfront bar so dingy and seedy that the walls seemed to sprout green bilge mushrooms. There were several dark booths, but the seats were so shredded they could not be used. I had seen—and often enjoyed patronizing—some downscale taverns in my drinking days, but nothing like this.

Peter marched us over to the bar, where the grim-faced bartender, who seemed to have successfully avoided any contact with the sun since 1945, looked at us in stupefaction.

A derelict at the end of the bar roused himself sufficiently to wail, "It's the Salvation Army."

This, for some reason, angered Lucy, who retorted, "Young man"—he was at least ten years older than she—"I have no interest whatsoever in your soul."

The wake commenced. There was no air-conditioning; only three slow-motion overhead fans.

Peter ordered beer for all and several bags of pretzels. The beer, leaving aside its taste, was almost cold. The steins almost clean. The pretzels almost crisp enough to chew.

Timothy seemed to get smashed after only a few swigs. Isobel said she didn't care for the beer, and when she reached down to get one of her imported cans from her omnipresent cooler, John restrained her in a kindly fashion.

You know those fabled wakes where drunken camaraderie and fellowship reign? This wasn't one of them. No songs were sung. No testimonials to the deceased were delivered. In fact, no one said a word.

Then, without warning, Peter shouted, "It's over! It's all over!" meaning, I supposed, the ceremony, the wake. But perhaps he meant something more. Perhaps he meant his life was over. Surely, Teresa Aguilar's life was over.

We filed out.

I heard Lucy ask Peter as we all headed east,

"Tell me, in that wondrous land where you met Teresa—with those vultures allergic to carrion— were they black vultures or turkey vultures?"

He did not answer her question. All he said was, "I shall be there tomorrow morning."

At Eleventh Avenue Timothy said good-bye and headed downtown. When we reached Tenth Avenue the group, excepting me, of course—I was now only a stone's throw from my West Side apartment—flagged a cab and piled in. Well, Lucy lingered for a moment at my side.

"Would you like to come home with me and reason with Duke?" I asked. "We could have some iced tea."

"Not now, Markus."

"Believe me, Lucy, my motives are pure."

"I'm sure they are. But the answer is still no."

I pouted a little.

"Markus, do you by chance remember that old song 'Nature Boy'?"

"Yes."

"Do you think he exists?"

"Who? Nat King Cole? Or did you mean the Johnny Ray version of the song?"

"No, Markus. I mean Nature Boy himself."

"I don't know. After all, Peter claims he met

that woman in some mythical land where the vultures are vegetarians."

"Forget Peter. Think, Marcus. Is it possible there exists a young man who wanders Central Park with a folding table and champagne just in case he happens upon a wedding?"

"You mean a desperado of kindness? A sweet Scarlet Pimpernel?"

"How nicely put, Markus."

She didn't give me a chance to really answer the question. She vanished into a yellow cab and I trudged back to my apartment to face the three-legged terrorist.

By 7:05 A.M. the next morning almost everyone had gathered again.

Peter had assured us that he would be there—but there was no sign of him.

Lucy urged, "Markus, please call Peter now. Maybe he overslept. We won't wait much longer."

"I don't have a quarter," I said.

Timothy not only volunteered a coin but also volunteered to make the call. He loped across the avenue on those endless legs of his and used the pay phone. In what seemed only seconds, he was loping back with his report.

"He's not there. The machine answered. Said he was on a short vacation. Leave a message, it said. I didn't."

"Well," Isobel declared enthusiastically, "that's the first intelligent thing that poor man has done in a while. If there is one person who needs a vacation, it's him."

We all agreed and headed into the park. Lucy took us north on the horse path (some people call it the bridle path), along the reservoir, following the path as it veered west and then ultimately south.

We concentrated on the heavily brambled slopes running up from the horse path to the cinder track just adjacent to the reservoir.

But the early downward migration of the northern birds seemed to have been canceled.

Oh, we saw a few kinds of warblers, a red-eyed vireo, and a kingbird family. But that was all. Given what we were expecting, it was a bummer, as I once heard Timothy say. We weren't in synch with ourselves or each other or the park. Maybe it was because of the recent tragedy.

Anyway, Lucy understood and we camped for

an early lunch. Not in our usual spot—which was where Teresa Aguilar was murdered—but in the now overgrown and untended Shakespeare Garden, just west of the Belvedere castle.

After the hard-boiled eggs and oranges and crackers; after Isobel had consumed two cans of her imported brew; and after I had performed my main function as an Olmsted's Irregular (garbageman with plastic bag), we set out again.

This time Lucy led us into the heart of the Ramble and to the beautiful structure called the Ramble Arch.

Hidden in the denser trees and shrubs of the west side of the Ramble, this rough stone structure is in a cleft between two high outcroppings of rock. The sun rarely reaches it during summer because of the foliage. Shafts of light filter down on it and the path it straddles, creating a space of mystery and beauty.

The arch is only five feet across, but the passageway is nine feet long.

The genius who created Central Park was a disciplined man. But in the Ramble—in his desire to create an idealized native woodland—he went a little bananas.

What he really created was a garden of Dionysus. In spite of the fact that most of the fauna is native to the Americas, one cannot stand in the intense bucolic Ramble, particularly around the arch, with the sound of the nearby stream gurgling on, and not feel that one has been transported to a sylvan glade in ancient Greece . . . and that the maenads with their flutes are about to appear and begin their seductive, savage dances.

Yes, we all just stood there before the arch, drinking in the pregnant stillness, broken by rustling, running water, crackling twigs—but always returning to a hush.

Please forgive me for the purple prose. I am usually a man of understatement, reason. But . . . ah . . . the Ramble does derange me on occasion.

Irrepressible Isobel, however, began to point out several bushes and trees: a hackberry, a white mulberry, a silver bell, a horse chestnut, and several "cucumber" trees with their strange mottled coppery bark.

Suddenly, as she was speaking, there came over the group a palpable unease. Something was very wrong. Some kind of discordant element had emerged.

That element was Lucy. She was standing absolutely still, as if transfixed, her eyes half open.

No! Not absolutely still. In fact, she was swaying slightly, like a cobra. Her strange posture seemed to disturb the air. I could see the beads of sweat on her lovely cheekbones.

Had she gone into some kind of trance?

Isobel fell silent and looked to me for guidance. I could give none.

Then Lucy very slowly raised one hand and pointed toward one of the stone supports of the arch, which was wreathed in brambles with a healthy admixture of trash.

The Ramble, being one of the more isolated areas of the park but easily accessible, is often used by unsavory individuals for sloppy trysts, particularly at night.

Lucy pulled in a deep breath. We all did. Our eyes strained on the point like bird dogs. What the hell was she pointing at? The tension was well nigh unbearable.

And then the owl materialized. We saw it in waves. First John, then Timothy and I, and finally Isobel, who let out what could only be called a groan of pleasure.

Seated on a confluence of rock, crushed juice

containers, and raised tree roots was an immature barn owl.

Even I could tell that it was a barn owl. I recognized the dishlike face, large eyes, and peculiar ears.

Now, there are owls in Central Park and there are barn owls among them. But they aren't often seen at this time of year or at this time of day.

And sightings of immature owls of any sort are rare at any time.

We stood pinned to the spot, making no sounds.

The young owl blinked and blinked but did not move except for one quick dip into its feathers with its beak.

I looked at Lucy. She was glowing like an incandescent bulb.

I alone of the Irregulars knew why . . . understood her almost rapturous response to the creature.

I alone of the Olmsted's Irregulars knew that Lucy Wayles, although born a good Southern Baptist, believed herself to have been an owl in some past life.

She had never actually confessed this belief in

those words. But I had put two and two together during several conversations with her.

Once, when I had asked her how she was able to cut through complex problems so quickly and elegantly, she replied that she merely followed the example of the hunting owl.

Pressed to elaborate, she said, "I hunt at night. I gather in all possible sounds. The computer in my brain processes those sounds and sends a signal to my talons so that they are automatically aligned with the mouse—I mean the problem."

I thought at the time that she was joshing me, but subsequent comments about owls taught me otherwise.

Anyway, we basked in the owl's gaze (they always look a little stupid to me) for a short time and then Lucy signaled that it was time to go.

We tiptoed out of the sylvan glade.

The sighting had made our day. We walked happily toward the place where we had assembled earlier.

Lucy was humming. I thought I even caught a tear sliding down from one of her lovely eyes. Maybe she thought that little barn owl was a long-lost cousin. Who knows?

And as we approached the exit to the park, she

certainly did what could be construed as a pirouette.

What would she have done, I began to wonder, if it had been a great horned owl blinking at us on that tree stump. A tremor of excitement went through me.

We tarried a bit longer together than usual because it was Friday and we would not gather again until Monday—weekends we gave the park back to the nonaffiliated—and because the little owl had so enchanted us.

Even Timothy was a bit high from the sighting. He whispered to me, "Did you ever notice that it is difficult to determine the nature of the prey from the appearance of the predator?"

I was chewing on that, intellectually, when I heard Lucy announce: "I have a good idea."

Now, I have heard her make that innocent comment hundreds of times. How was I to know that this time it would have deep ramifications?

Then she said, "No doubt Peter is taking a very short vacation. He'll be back shortly. Maybe even momentarily. Let us show him we care for him and miss him."

There were murmurs of assent.

"Will you do that for us, Markus?"

"Do what, Lucy?"

"Get him some beautiful flowers and lay them with a card in front of his door . . . so that the first thing he sees when he returns will be the flowers from his companions."

She was laying it on a bit thick.

"Of course I will," I replied, rather unhappy about the assignment.

"And on Monday, Markus, we will all reimburse you. Remember to save the bill."

There was no way out. I headed downtown on Madison Avenue and purchased a huge bouquet of purple snapdragons laced with tiny yellow roses. The combination was both endearing and grotesque.

On the card I wrote: *Condolences. The Olmsted's Irregulars.*

Then, realizing this was not supposed to be a condolence bouquet but a companionship one—I ripped the card up and penned another one: *Welcome Home. From Olmsted's Irregulars.*

Then I headed for Peter's place on Seventy-third Street. He told us that he had purchased the brownstone, just off Madison Avenue, for a song years ago. He had gutted and rebuilt it to make his triplex apartment, or studio, as it was called.

I turned the corner and stopped in front of the house. Nope, I realized, wrong building. I walked on. Then turned back, then crossed over, then crossed back, then became totally confused.

What was the matter with me? I couldn't find the house. Alzheimer's? Sclerosis? Sunstroke?

I walked back to Madison. Start over, I told myself. Go slowly.

Then my native analytical powers kicked in. Wait a minute, they urged.

I had seen the house and passed it by. Hadn't I?

My head guided my feet back to Seventy-third Street.

Yes! That is Peter Marin's place. Right in front of me.

But now it was understandable why I had not recognized it.

One side of the house, on the lower level, was charred and boarded up.

No. Not construction work. There had been a fire. A very recent fire.

An hour later, twenty blocks uptown, Lucy and I stood on the street in front of her abode.

From the street I could look into her apartment

window and see Dipper's sneering face. I believe he was hissing at me.

The moment I had informed Lucy of the fire, she set the wheels in motion.

"Come here immediately, Markus," she ordered. "And while waiting I shall demand an explanation from the fire department—or Peter, if he is back."

The fire people hung up on her. Peter's number was busy. If indeed he had come back from his little respite, he was talking to someone. Getting repair estimates? Talking to his insurance agent?

Frustrated, Lucy had called the NYPD. She had told them she must speak to Detectives Rupp and Halkin.

Obviously the message was garbled because when Rupp pulled up in his unmarked car and rolled down the window, he said, "I hope you got something important for me."

Obviously he had interrupted something more crucial or pleasurable to visit us, in the belief we had valuable information on the Aguilar murder.

"No, young man," Lucy informed him, "I hope you have something important for me concerning the fire at Peter Marin's home. You do remember who Peter Marin is, don't you? The intended groom of the murdered girl."

A look of disbelief shrouded Detective Rupp's honest blunt face. He shot out of the vehicle in a fury, slamming the door shut and stomping around while the smoke blew like a train whistle from his ears.

When he had calmed himself, he asked Lucy evenly, quite mildly, "Do you mean to tell me that you left that 'urgent' message for me and Halkin to get over here so that we could fill you in on the details of a small house fire?"

"Yes," she answered simply, equally sweet.

"Well, of course, your majesty. Sorry we didn't contact you last night at two a.m. when the inferno started. Several young people on the way home from a concert in the park had a bit too much to drink and a few too many of those funny cigarettes and climbed through a half-open window in the basement of a brownstone. One of them left a cigarette burning. It ignited a pile of newspapers stacked in the corner waiting to be recycled. A neighbor noticed the smoke and called it in. The whole thing was over in a few minutes. Not very much damage."

He looked expectantly at Lucy then. And just

to make certain we understood how biting his sarcasm was, he added: "I hope my report meets with your satisfaction, your majesty. Was it complete enough for you? Any unanswered questions?"

"Just one," Lucy said. "Are you sure it wasn't arson—that the fire wasn't set deliberately?"

"No accelerant was used, Miss Wayles."

"I see. Well, thank you so much, Detective Rupp."

"And now may I return to my duties—my other duties, that is—your majesty?"

"By all means, Detective."

He climbed into the car and took off.

Lucy turned to me then. "What happened to those flowers, Markus?"

I slapped my forehead in consternation. "I . . . uh . . . don't . . ."

I had to let that sentence trail off. I had no idea what had become of my welcome home bouquet. "I must have left them somewhere in all the excitement," I had to confess.

"It's time to gather them in," she replied.

"But I just told you, I don't know what I did with them."

"I don't mean the flowers, Markus. I mean the Irregulars."

"Oh. Why?"

"Let's just make the calls, Markus."

"But, Lucy, we just left the park a few hours ago. Won't everyone be tired?"

"Nonsense. I'll make iced tea and serve them ham and cheese sandwiches, very thin sandwiches, the proper way. I think I must have *some* meat in the cooler. Perhaps with a piece of lettuce."

I knew it was futile to remonstrate.

Five hours after we had seen that blinking owl in the Ramble, the Olmsted's Irregulars regathered, this time in Lucy's apartment.

It turned out she did not have the makings for those sandwiches, thinness aside. And in fact she had run out of tea bags.

Lucy called us to order. "Thank you for coming on such short notice. Let's get right down to business, shall we?" She looked around the room but did not wait for the group's assent to that rhetorical question. "There was a fire early this morning at Peter Marin's."

"What?" Isobel burst out. "Was he hurt?"

"It was a small fire," Lucy said. "Little damage resulted. So little, in fact, that the phone lines were not even affected. If you recall, Timothy called him this morning and Peter's vacation message was intact. No, no one was hurt, Isobel. And maybe Peter has already come back by now. We all know he takes one-day vacations when he takes them at all."

John interrupted her. "I remember he once took a three-day vacation—with a woman."

"Yes. Well, he might be back and he might not be back. Let us leave things at that. The police say the fire was accidental. That some young people were where they should not have been, doing things they should not have been doing, including being careless with their cigarettes."

Lucy stopped speaking and looked around at all of us, a shepherd doting on her flock.

"Surely you haven't called us together again for this bulletin?" John asked tartly.

Lucy replied grandly, "I have assembled you here because it is time, I believe, to resurrect the investigative apparatus of Olmsted's Irregulars."

I heard John groan.

Isobel and Timothy looked confused. They didn't know that Olmsted's Irregulars were really a clone of the Baker Street Irregulars. They thought we were strictly a bird-watching group.

I shared in their puzzlement. But I didn't know why. I should have seen this development coming.

"What, precisely, is to be investigated?" Wu inquired.

Lucy's answering sigh seemed to encompass the four sides of the apartment, indeed the world.

"I do believe our dear friend Peter Marin is caught in a web of violence and duplicity from which he will not emerge . . . alive . . . without our help. I also do believe that the moment we can identify the shape of the web strangling poor Peter we will know why Teresa Aguilar was murdered and by whom."

Well! That certainly was a mouthful. We were all staring dumbly at her.

"Following that course of reason," she continued, "I propose we immediately start a surveillance of Peter. Perhaps Timothy and Markus will be the initial team. Perhaps this team will assemble as early as tomorrow morning."

"Wait a minute! Just wait a minute!" John shouted.

"Yes, dear?"

"Lucy, do you have any real evidence that Peter is in trouble? I mean beyond the fact that he has lost his would-be wife and his equilibrium."

"This web is sticky, John. It leaves sensations rather than quantifiable facts at this time."

"Listen, Lucy, you're not making any sense."

"Oh? Enlighten me."

"Okay. Sure I will. Granted that the Irregulars played a key role in solving two murders in the past. But remember, the victims were a bird-watcher and a bird artist, respectively. They inhabited our world, our milieu. And there were suspects—a whole lot of them. Many of them we even knew personally, or knew of them. The murder of Teresa Aguilar is a whole different ball game. We don't know anything about her and there are no viable suspects. This is the kind of murder only the police can handle. They dig out random facts one by one. They question her neighbors, find out about old lovers. Ferret out motives for the murder. It's called building a case. They search her apartment, read her old shopping lists or whatever. It's cold, relentless legwork, and it's called police procedure. It works, Lucy, and it's been working for hundreds of years now.

"Agatha Christie and Ruth Rendell and Sue Grafton and even the great Sherlock are, if you'll pardon the expression, like rubes playing the commodities exchange in these kinds of crimes. Face facts, Lucy. We don't know police procedure. We can't *do* procedure."

I thought he made an excellent presentation. I wanted to applaud.

Timothy gestured that he wanted to say something to me out of earshot of the others. I leaned over, keeping my eye on Dipper, who was staring at me malevolently from the top of the refrigerator.

Here is what he asked me: "Do you really believe there are storms on the sun that last for seventy thousand years?"

I whispered back, "I'll have to think about it."

For some reason John Wu's analytical discourse seemed to have discombobulated Isobel. She hemmed and hawed and muttered and glared. Then she crushed out her cigarette, stood up, and pointed an accusing finger at Wu.

She said in a loud, stentorian voice, "Watchman! Whither has the sparrow flown?"

Then she sat down.

"Thank you, Isobel, for reminding us of that lovely old Lutheran hymn," said Lucy. "It was, I believe, often sung at the gravesite of a child. Now, to get on with the matter at hand: We are all agreed, aren't we? Surveillance will begin at dawn tomorrow."

Chapter 6

What do surveillance teams eat for breakfast? It was on my mind. And what do children like Timothy—he couldn't have been more than twenty-five—eat for breakfast? All this was on my mind after the alarm woke me at 5 A.M.

I decided that I would place five eggs in boiling water at 5:55 A.M. Timothy was due at six. I would medium boil the eggs, take them out at 5:59, and then lay them in their shells on a plate, along with rye bread slices, butter, and cherry jam.

As the hour ticked ferociously toward Timothy's ETA, I realized there was a much more dangerous problem facing me than breakfast.

I shuddered just thinking about it.

What if one or more of the DEA agents in the shootout with Duke's drug-dealing owner (should I call him a patron? a companion? teacher?) were African-Americans?

And what if Duke, when he saw Timothy enter the apartment, experienced a violent flashback and suddenly thought the DEA in the person of Timothy was there to blow him away?

And what if he then attacked the unsuspecting Timothy?

Oh, my. This was a severe problem.

I realized that the only safe thing to do was either 1) lock Duke in his bedroom or 2) stay close to Timothy from the moment he entered, and if Duke launched a preemptive strike, quickly push Timothy back through the door and out of harm's way.

I liked the first idea but Duke was already in the living room. How was I going to persuade him to go back into his room? Trickery. But it was dangerous, I felt, to play a trick on Duke.

So I took the second option and, as soon as the eggs were done, took up my post by the door.

At six a.m. sharp the doorman rang up to inform me that a young man named Timothy was just entering the elevator.

I waited by the door. Duke was snoozing about five feet away.

A knock. I opened the door slowly and narrowly.

"Good morning, Markus."

"To you too," I said. "Would you care for some breakfast?"

"Sure."

I let him in a few inches at a time, keeping my eye on Duke.

But the beast simply opened one eye, once, regarded the visitor opaquely, and then resumed his snooze. I removed all restraint. The tall young man strode into the center of the living room, pushed his glasses against the bridge of his nose, and looked around.

Then he looked at the dog, circled him, and said, "I see you have a three-legged pit bull."

I liked the way he stated it; as if a three-legged pit bull were a distinct breed . . . as if one bred and showed three-legged pit bulls in a separate category at the Westminster Kennel Club.

"That's right," I replied. "Lucy obtained him for me." I decided to leave out the fact that I adopted him under duress.

We sat down in the kitchen for breakfast.

Timothy was wearing below the knee shorts and a faded red polo shirt on which was printed in large letters: ALASKA.

After he peeled, peppered, salted, and ate his first egg, he asked, "Where's the Batmobile?"

It took me a while to realize he was talking, in a humorous vein, about the car I was renting for the surveillance assignment.

"We'll pick it up on Fifty-fourth Street. Hertz."

He nodded. Timothy looked weary, which was understandable. He probably got off his night job at the restaurant only a few hours ago.

I truly liked this strange science fiction writer cum waiter cum bird-watcher. I wondered if he looked upon me as a surrogate grandfather or generic uncle.

We totally consumed the surveillance breakfast except for a few rye bread crusts that Timothy fed to Duke. Then we left the apartment, picked up a small rental car (a Geo), and, with Timothy at the wheel, drove to Madison Avenue at Seventy-third Street, where he parked at a corner meter.

We had an unobstructed view of Peter Marin's abode.

The hunt was on, if indeed the fox was back

from vacation. If not, we hounds would appear quite dim-witted.

It was a warm morning. Traffic—both foot and vehicular—was sparse. We opened all the windows in the car. Timothy fell fast asleep behind the wheel. I just sat there, feeling quite silly in my surveillance role. It dawned on me that I ought to put a quarter in the meter, but I didn't. I daydreamed about Lucy and me on a sailing ship, dressed as pirates.

The fox came out of his den at eight-fifteen wearing a slouch hat, Bermuda shorts that were too tight, and a rayon shirt patterned with cavorting dolphins. I shook Timothy awake.

Peter was carrying a strange-looking large canvas bag. It seemed to be the kind artists use to transport their canvases. It was heavy, apparently. He moved slowly.

Timothy started the engine. Peter walked to Fifth Avenue and boarded the first bus that came along.

This was not expected. It is very hard to follow a New York City bus in another vehicle. But we did it, moving slowly in the left lane while the bus was in the right, keeping about a hundred feet behind the behemoth.

Our success of course was to a great extent due to my constant advice to the driver. The very light Saturday morning traffic might have played a minor role.

Peter and bag exited the bus at Twenty-third Street and headed west to Sixth Avenue. Then he turned uptown and entered one of the huge flea markets on the east side of the avenue.

We parked the car and began following him. I was astonished at how many flea markets there now were on Sixth Avenue on weekends. Virtually every parking lot had booths, stands, sheds, tents, and racks selling everything from furniture to jewelry to clothing to books to military medals to antique watches.

"Istanbul," Timothy whispered to no one in particular.

Even the sidewalks and doorways of stores and buildings were occupied by vendors. And even though it was only 9 A.M. there were throngs of browsers and shoppers.

We stayed about fifty feet behind Peter. His bulk and hat were always visible.

He stopped at a booth that sold prints, posters, and reproductions of paintings.

There was a brief conversation with a small

bearded gentleman who manned the booth. Then Peter unzipped the bag and pulled out two items. They appeared to be framed posters. Money changed hands. Peter pocketed the cash and strode out, passing not ten feet from us. He was in a kind of daze.

"This is serious," I remarked worriedly to Timothy.

"That Lucy Wayles is titanium," he replied. By which I assumed he was verifying my claim of seriousness—and paying Lucy a compliment.

We walked to the booth. I studied the items Peter had just sold. It was a very sad moment for me. They were large framed reproductions of two of his more famous public service advertisements . . . one for Earth Day and one for AIDS research.

They had been presented to him at an annual awards dinner of the Advertising Council of New York.

"How much?" I inquired of the small bearded man, pointing to the Earth Day poster, which depicted in a whimsical manner a family of garter snakes waiting to cross an interstate highway chock-full of exhaust-belching trucks. All the snakes in the family were wearing oxygen masks and an old grandma snake was carrying an umbrella against the acid rain.

"Two hundred," the vendor said.

I felt a twinge in my heart. The vendor's asking price meant Peter must have sold it for only about a hundred dollars.

"Thank you," I said. "I'll be back."

I told Timothy, "Call Lucy. Have her meet us at the car as soon as she can. Tell her where we're parked."

A half hour later Lucy and Isobel slipped into the backseat. I was now at the wheel with Timothy beside me.

I detailed the bare facts our surveillance had disclosed.

"Excellent work," said Lucy. "It appears that Peter is in a severe cash crunch."

"But I thought he was a rich and famous commercial artist," said Isobel. Then she added, "At least that's what John hinted at."

"Where is John?" I asked.

"Brooding," answered Lucy.

"Maybe he blew it on fast women and slow horses," Isobel mused. "I mean, before he met Teresa. After all, the man does have those hooded eyes—like a compulsive gambler's."

That I never noticed. I myself bet on the horses from time to time. And my eyes are a bit blurry, but definitely not "hooded."

Lucy seemed to drift off into one of her intellectual trances.

We all sat there, uncomfortable. Finally she said, "The pool has become a bit clearer."

No one knew what to make of that. To me it seemed the pool was, if anything, murkier.

She leaned over and said, "I think, Markus, you should take Timothy to breakfast. The boy needs some weight on him."

"We've already had breakfast, Lucy. I made it."

She waved her hand scornfully, as if my meals could not be taken seriously. Sometimes Lucy can be cruel to me.

"You must take Timothy to that new place for donuts on Twenty-third Street. I think it has a name like Krispus Abscondus. Timothy needs sustenance. He is quite thin."

"What about you and Isobel?"

"We have a bit of women's work to do. We shall join you in about an hour. Enjoy your donuts and wait for us."

So I squired Timothy to the donut shop. We

watched the hot, sugary things roll out of the oven in ranks, like soldiers of the queen.

There were only seven varieties. One would think the selection would be easy. On the contrary. Timothy seemed dazzled and perplexed by the choices.

Finally he ordered one of each of five varieties—the donuts, to be fair, were small—and a glass of milk.

I chose a jelly donut and a cup of coffee and we repaired to a table.

Timothy began surgery on his donuts, cutting each one in half fastidiously. Then he looked at his handiwork.

"Now there are ten!" he announced in delight. I wondered if he was one of those fanatics who got drunk when he was in proximity to fresh donuts. I'd known people like that.

I watched him eat half of one donut, then half of a different one. Then it was time for a gulp of the milk.

I pierced the skin of the jelly donut.

"You know," Timothy said wistfully, "I believe artificial intelligence as personified by the computer will eventually surpass human intelligence. And that this artificial intelligence will develop a form of consciousness."

"No, Timothy. I was not aware you believed that."

He attacked a glazed donut half. "Then and only then," he said, "will some of the more perplexing riddles of existence be solved."

"Riddles?"

"Yes. Like why the rose grows in a dung heap but not in an Italian marble quarry."

Hmmm. I nibbled at my donut.

"Or why," he continued, "the rose is so beautiful but its roots so ugly."

"Yes," I agreed, "those are disturbing questions."

He and I were silent for a long time after that. He consumed all the donuts during the lull.

Then he looked at me fiercely.

"Oh, there are so many riddles. Endless riddles. For example, if generation upon generation of bird-watchers have confirmed that the male house sparrow suffers from satyriasis and the female from nymphomania—how come there are so few of them left in the Bronx?"

I mulled that one over for a while. I was about

to propose a tentative solution when—suddenly—I saw a vision.

At least for a moment I thought it was a vision. Two women had entered the shop.

One was Isobel Soba. Of that I was sure.

The other was—perhaps—Lucy Wayles.

Or was it a bird of paradise? Or a Caribbean bombshell?

Was she walking toward me, or dancing? The merengue?

No. It was a genuine vision. Definitely Lucy Wayles. And then she was standing right in front of me. I cannot describe the dress she wore. It was a light yellow one, long, with puff sleeves and a riot of red and black ruffles about the bosom (or does one say the bodice) and the bottom hem.

"Do you like it, Markus?" she asked.

"You'd better like it," said Isobel. "It's a Teresa Aguilar creation."

I was flabbergasted. I heard Timothy whisper, "Titanium!"

Lucy took a seat and immediately launched into her monologue.

"We found this dress in what purported to be an antique clothing booth. Teresa made it. It's one of several the vendor had purchased from her over the past few years for resale. Then Teresa suddenly stopped bringing her clothes around. That was about six months ago. We can now assume that it was in that very flea market that Peter met her. Perhaps he refused to reveal as much to us because he considers flea markets tawdry. Ah . . . so many desperate men, so few brains. A flea market could never be tawdry. Am I correct, Markus? To meet one's true love in a flea market is a blessed event. Isn't that true, Markus?"

I didn't get the chance to answer. She continued in a harsh tone: "Business! Let's get down to business. Teresa Aguilar, several months ago, began to sell her clothing elsewhere. Out of the flea markets and into the boutiques where she was no doubt receiving more money for her creations. Perhaps to help Peter, who we now know is, for whatever reason, on a slide into penury. With all this in mind, I hope I have parceled out the assignments fairly."

"What assignments?" I asked.

"You, Markus, will cover the boutiques and ladies shops on the Upper West Side. Take Timothy along to control your asperity. I shall handle the West Village. Isobel will take the Lexington and Madison Avenue boutiques. And if John has recovered from his pouting, he can handle the Lower East Side."

"But Teresa lived in Queens," I pointed out. "Who'll go there?"

"Don't be an idiot," Isobel quipped. "Dress prices in Queens are permanently depressed."

Then Lucy looked down in horror at the remains of the donut repast.

"Shame on you, Markus, taking young Timothy into a place like this for breakfast. Couldn't you have found a more healthful place to eat?"

I knew it was useless to argue. I changed the subject back to procedure.

"When are we to begin these assignments?" I asked.

"Monday morning. Instead of the usual seven a.m. gathering, we will meet at two in the afternoon, at the Bethesda Fountain."

"But what if Peter shows up as usual?"

"Markus, Markus, Markus," she said regretfully. "You have eyes but you do not see. Peter has withdrawn. He is in crisis—*crises*, that is. He has many of them at present. He is crippled. He is like a wounded beast. We can only help him from a distance. As I've already told you, he has been caught in circumstances. But we cannot discern the pattern yet—the glue—or the possibility of escape. Let us simply perform our tasks with diligence."

She stood up suddenly, flung her arms out, and said, "Now I must change. This dress is a bit outré for a woman of my age. Is that not so, Markus?"

She pirouetted out of the donut shop. I was mute.

Chapter 7

No one will ever know the abuse I suffered on that morning expedition to the boutiques of the Upper West Side.

Originally I had thought Lucy to be overzealous in her cancellation of our usual outing. I mean why not bird-watch a few early morning hours in the park and then go on our assignments?

After three boutique visits, I realized her wisdom. It was exhausting work . . . from one to the other with Timothy in tow.

No one seemed to know what I was talking about. No one had heard of or purchased a garment for resale from Teresa Aguilar.

Worse still, the shopkeepers were suspicious and unfriendly. They treated me like a gardener treats a bluejay, keeping it under close surveillance so it doesn't abscond with the choice berries. Imagine a man of my age, station, and intelligence being treated in such a manner.

As I said, it is too painful to tell the whole sordid story. Anyway, by 2 P.M. Timothy and I had arrived at Bethesda Fountain. Lucy and John were already there. I immediately reported to the commander that the mission had been a total failure.

Lucy was consoling.

"You tried, Markus. That's all I asked. Neither I nor John had any success either."

"What next?"

"Let's wait for Isobel before we decide," she said.

I suddenly realized how strange it was to be in the park at that hour. Everything seemed different. In the early morning hours Central Park was tentative, exciting, unfinished, foggy. But in the afternoon it was a bit stultifying. Like a postcard. And the heat . . . aah, that August heat.

Lucy pointed. "Here comes Isobel," she announced.

Indeed, it was Isobel approaching from the east, puffing on a cigarette and striding without fear on the Seventy-second Street bypass road between cyclists, joggers, roller bladers, and occasional vehicles.

When she reached us, we knew she had something. She flailed her stubby arms and said, "May I remind you all once again of Psalm Ninety-one. The Lord, the psalmist says, will send his angel to protect you. And I quote directly: 'Lest you dash your foot against a stone.' Believe me, I dashed no foot into anything other than pay dirt."

She dumped her cigarette and pulled a crumpled piece of paper from somewhere. She read it with clarity.

"Helen Bells is the name of both the boutique owner and the boutique itself. It is located on Eighty-third Street, just off Lexington."

She crumpled the paper and then added, "And yes, Helen Bells sells Teresa Aguilar fashions."

We didn't waste time congratulating her. We descended en masse on Helen Bells.

It was a lovely, high-ceilinged, narrow shop cluttered with garments, accessories, and knick-knacks.

Miss Bells was lovely, also. She showed us the

seven or eight Aguilar dresses she stocked, and then burst into tears at the memory of Teresa.

She had seen the TV reports on the murder. Yes, she had. And she was appalled.

Helen Bells suddenly had to sit down. John Wu rushed out to the corner deli and bought bottled water for her; Isobel fanned her with a magazine and Lucy held her hand.

She was a tall, narrow-hipped woman, this Helen Bells, with very short gray hair. She was wearing sandals and shorts and a white silk shirt. She looked in a way like a long-lost cousin of Lucy's.

"I never knew she was going to be married," Helen Bells said. "She never said a word. But then again . . . why should she? The man she always came in with was not the man she was supposed to marry."

A chill descended upon us.

John Wu shot me a strange look. I assumed he was confirming the efficacy of a procedural investigation . . . how if one searches enough, even randomly, something will pop out of someone's closet—or grave.

"Are you sure about this?" Lucy asked Helen.

"Yes. The man she often showed up with in

my store was definitely not the one they showed on the television screen as her fiancé. Different looks altogether."

"What was the name of the man she brought here so often?" Lucy probed.

"Armand."

"And his last name?"

Helen shook her head. "She never mentioned his last name. And he never said a word. All I know is, she called him Armand. He was a physician. I remember her telling me that. And he was small, wiry, and dark. They were engaged to be married, she said."

"When did you last see this Armand?" Lucy pressed.

"Maybe six months ago."

"You said he never talked. Why was that?"

"I don't really know. He seemed nervous though. Always silent and on edge."

"Is there anything else you can tell us about him?"

"Not really, no. Or about her."

"Anything," Lucy urged. "Anything at all."

"Well . . . this can't be the kind of thing you want to know, I'm sure, but . . . he always wore a beret. Not the usual kind of beret. And not worn in the usual way, pulled down on the side of the head. No, his was worn front to back."

"How old would you say he is?"

"I couldn't tell. But he was handsome, I'll say that. Perhaps also he was just shy. Perhaps that's why he never spoke. He was a sweet, shy person."

Helen Bells could think of nothing further to tell us. Lucy purchased a beach hat from her, though Lucy never goes to the beach. Isobel bought a pair of dress gloves. For the opera? John bought a little wooden box, for his niece, he said.

Timothy and I kept our hands in our pockets.

As our visit ended, Helen Bells cried out, "Who are you people? Are you a choral society? Did Teresa sing with you?"

As we exited the boutique, I realized my error. Helen Bells looked nothing at all like Lucy. She was in fact broader and shorter than I had originally thought. She looked sort of like a distant cousin of mine.

Then the entire Olmsted's Irregulars, sans Peter of course, marched to an air-conditioned bagel emporium on Third Avenue. We sat down at a large round table. Timothy took the order. John Wu supplied the funds.

Isobel was quite hungry. She asked for an "everything" bagel with scallion cream cheese. The rest of us ordered moderately. All of us had iced coffee or tea. The day was slipping away.

John Wu declared, "It is obvious to me that this Armand had Teresa murdered in a fit of jealous rage. All the facts seem to confirm a rejected suitor thesis."

Isobel said, "What does it matter what is obvious to you, John? This Armand is a cipher. All we know is that he is a small shy dark handsome physician. That's all. No plumage at all. If we could find him, we wouldn't know him. Hell, John, you couldn't even identify a yellow-breasted chat."

Lucy defused the situation with a simple question to John: "What do you think happened to Peter Marin's money?"

"How should I know?" he replied.

"Well, John," Lucy explained, "you are the man we turn to when we need information on all matters of finance."

"I'm merely a broker," he said modestly. "I'm not the Federal Reserve chairman. And my knowledge of Peter's finances is slight. But if you want me to speculate—if you'll pardon the expression—I will. I think what happened to Peter is quite common in the creative sphere. Peter was a sought-after commercial artist for many years. He was paid top dollar. He earned a great deal of money. Suddenly the work dried up. Peter thought it only a temporary state. In fact, the times had passed him by. He couldn't be frugal. And he couldn't get any of those big fees anymore. Suddenly the bottom dropped out. You wake up one morning and you're dead broke."

"That makes sense," I said.

"Thank you."

Isobel said, "The way I see it, a man going broke is no mystery at all. This Armand is the real mystery."

A strangely innocent look came over Lucy's face.

"Actually," she announced, "this Armand does not present much of a problem."

"Are you serious? He's *the* problem," said John.

"I don't think so," Lucy replied. "Someone like Markus could identify and locate him in a jiffy.

After all, Markus himself is a physician. Isn't that true, Markus?"

I cringed.

Lucy smiled her wonderful smile. Everyone else just looked perplexed.

"For example," Lucy proceeded, "I know Markus would take into account this Armand's shyness. Markus would immediately intuit that Armand was not cut out for private practice. Those kinds of physicians have to be loquacious. And given Armand's Latin first name and the strong possibility that he is a foreign national, Markus would suggest that he works for a large medical institution of some kind. Markus knows that our hospitals and clinics and foundations are staffed with a great many foreign physicians."

There was silence in the bagel emporium. The poppy seeds were lying low. Would I really know all that?

Lucy went on. "And Markus, who has a keen eye for clothing and fashion, and the roots of fashion, would immediately intuit where Armand got that style of beret wearing. Markus keeps up on world affairs. He knows the United

Nations peacekeeping forces are known to wear their blue berets crushed down, front to back."

Everyone stared at me again. Was I brilliant?

Lucy continued, "See how easy it would be for Markus to find this Armand? He would know that Armand probably works for some kind of medical service organization attached to or affiliated with the U.N. Maybe funded by the Quakers or Catholic Charities or the World Council of Churches. Yes, Markus would know all this. And, dear man that he is, he would also know that my friend Constance is reference librarian at the New York Historical Society, only a few blocks from here; and that this Constance owes me not a few favors."

There was an astonished silence now.

"Yes," Lucy said after the long pause, with innocence, "for Markus, this Armand wouldn't be a problem at all."

So we left our half-finished bagels and walked to that august, elegant private library called the New York Historical Society, on Seventy-ninth Street and Madison Avenue.

And Constance, whom I had never laid eyes on before, though at first startled by the horde of bird-watchers, settled down.

She found, within eleven minutes of on-line directory searching, a physician named Armand Gratia who was associate director of something called Mercy Village.

This thing called Mercy Village was actually a consortium of progressive nurses and doctors funded by U.S. church groups under the aegis of the World Health Organization. Their main thrust? Nutritional deficiencies and communicable diseases. Their main locale? West Africa. Their headquarters? New York City.

"You are brilliant!" Isobel whispered passionately in my ear.

Was she drunk?

Chapter 8

I had been ordered to reveal the existence of Armand Gratia to the NYPD by Lucy, speaking on behalf of the Olmsted's Irregulars.

"It is the will of the people," Lucy declared.

So I didn't play around. I walked right into the spanking new police administration building attached to a very old precinct house in the vicinity of Columbus Avenue and Eighty-first Street.

It was late Monday evening.

In my hand I held a piece of paper on which was written the name, occupation, and affiliation of one Armand Gratia; and the New York City address of Mercy Village.

Detective Rupp was not there. Detective Halkin was. He was seated behind a low, rather ugly desk, wearing a white short-sleeved shirt and yellow tie. He was reading a brochure on new ferry services within the metropolitan area.

He did not greet me warmly. He did not, in fact, know who the hell I was until I recited certain code words that jogged his memory.

"Oh, yeah," he said.

I handed him the paper. He read it and then looked up at me. "So?"

I was not expecting such a response.

"Perhaps it would be worthwhile if you contacted this gentleman," was the best I could do.

"Look, pal. We already know about this guy. We already found him. We already talked to him. He's a doctor. One of those bleeding hearts who runs around the globe with aspirins. Married with a family. Had a hot affair with the deceased. But he's no suspect. He was in Africa at the time. And he broke off the thing with Teresa Aguilar months ago. No bad feelings between them. No nothing. Not even roller blades. You got anything else for me?"

"No," I said, a bit dazzled by what he knew.

"Well, I got something for you," he said. And he gestured that I should lean over the desk. I did.

"Listen. I've been a cop twenty-two years. And

a detective eleven years. I've seen a whole lot of mayhem. But I never heard of something this bizarre. A roller blader zooming down out of the blue and blowing away a bride-to-be in an outdoor ceremony. The fact is, pal, I don't believe it."

"But I was there, Detective. It happened," I replied, a bit angrily.

"It was a bird-watcher's wedding, wasn't it?"

"I guess you could call it that. I mean, the groom certainly was a bird-watcher."

"And the spectators?"

"Yes."

He gave me a nasty little grin. Oh, I thought, do not bird-watchers bleed? Do we not reason? Are we not part and parcel of humankind? Shall we not . . . ?

My bardlike silent improvisation ended abruptly.

"Come by anytime," he barked, "when you have something real for us."

I slunk out.

I rose at six the next morning, ready for another day's work as sanitation engineer of the Olmsted's Irregulars.

Outside it was pouring; a late summer deluge. But that was of no significance. We gathered no matter the weather or the state of the city or the world. Blackouts, storms, nuclear accidents— they are meaningless.

Usually I get out of bed quickly. But not that morning. A very strange memory came to me. A brief passionate affair. Long before I met Lucy. Twenty years ago. At a conference on cold viruses in London.

Her name was Tebrith. She was an Algerian national employed by a pharmaceutical lab in Switzerland. We met on the opening day of the conference. It was love at first sight. That very night we slept together. It was a delirious experience for me.

But at breakfast the next morning, she said, "This will not happen again."

"Why?" I literally cried out, not believing my ears.

She said, "I share with Baudelaire a sickening disgust with earthly experience that is essentially superficial."

At the time, I hadn't the slightest idea what she was talking about. Nor did I understand it twenty years later when the memory surfaced that rainy morning.

I blotted Tebrith out of my consciousness and swung my legs over the side of the bed.

There was another surprise waiting for me: Duke. He was not destroying my dress shoes this time. He was lying in the doorway with the end of a kitchen towel in his jaws; the rest of the towel was draped over his shoulder. He wasn't ripping the fabric; in fact, he was holding it rather gently. And he kept his eyes on me. That was the problem. Those eyes were mystifying that morning. I had the oddest sense that he was staring at me *with affection* . . . almost—dare I say it—with love.

I stepped over him gingerly, showered, dressed, and rushed uptown to the gathering place.

Once there, I counted umbrellas. Only four: mine, Lucy's, John's, and Isobel's.

"Where is Timothy?" Isobel asked.

None of us knew. Timothy had never once failed to show up since he joined the Irregulars.

"First Peter, now Timothy. Where will it end?" Isobel wailed.

"Peter called me last night," John said. "He

sends his best. He'll return as soon as he straightens his life out. Those were his words. I offered him a loan. He denied being in financial trouble. Poor, proud man."

The sky opened up. Usually we sheltered in the park until the weather cleared, but the downpour was now so horrific that Lucy led us across the avenue to the Guggenheim Museum a block south.

There we stood, under the ample ledge jutting out from the bookstore, sharing it with two dog walkers and a homeless man with a shopping cart full of bundles.

"We can't call Timothy," John noted. "He never gave us his telephone number or address. We don't even know his last name."

"The child has a right to his privacy," Lucy said sweetly.

"I'm not denying that right," John retorted. "I'm just noting a fact."

Isobel lit a cigarette and puffed furiously. The dog walkers, one accompanied by a chocolate Lab and the other by a collie mix, tried to move as far as possible from her without getting drenched.

Not only did the rain persist but it grew even

heavier. And with the sheets of water came lightning and thunder. We could see the streets beginning to flood.

Then it tapered off a bit, but it did not stop. The dog walkers abandoned the shelter. The shoeless man lay down.

Isobel pointed to the heavens. "A bad omen," she said.

"Nonsense," answered John.

"Then a portent," she amended.

"It's just rain! Rain is good!" John rebutted.

"Unless it doesn't stop. Then you have to build an ark," she shot back.

For some reason, I began to sing a little ditty:

> "It rained forty days and forty nights,
> And it didn't stop till Christmas,
> The only man who survived the flood
> Was long-legged Jack of Isthmus."

"Where does that come from?" John asked.

"I haven't the slightest idea," I replied. I was telling the truth.

"No matter, Markus," Lucy intervened kindly. "It was quite lovely."

I positively glowed.

Believe it or not, we huddled there for another ninety minutes, until the sun suddenly burst through a tepid drizzle.

"Let us proceed," said Lucy.

We rushed for the park entrance. The creatures were waiting.

Once inside, we pulled up short. A scarecrow blocked our way.

No! It wasn't a scarecrow at all, we realized. It was Timothy in a pancho. He was eating a peach.

"Sorry I'm late."

"No matter," Lucy assured him. "Come along now."

"Wait!" Timothy said. "Listen!"

What strange behavior. But we waited.

"I am late because I was in Sunnyside, Queens," he revealed. Then he added, cryptically, "I was listening to the denizens of a small coffee shop having breakfast."

"What is the sound of one pancake clapping?" quipped Isobel.

"They were talking about their neighbor Teresa Aguilar," Timothy said.

There was a pregnant, nervous silence.

Then Lucy asked, "Why did you go out there, Timothy?"

"To help, of course. To further the investigation into Death and the Maiden."

"And you heard something important?"

"Yes. I think very important."

John Wu gave a low, despairing groan. Isobel lit a cigarette. Lucy smiled. I fiddled with the heavy U.S. Navy surplus binoculars that hung at my neck.

Timothy began, "She owned a very strange vehicle. She kept it in an open lot in Long Island City. It was torched about the same time as the fire in Peter Marin's house."

"And the arsonists, Timothy?" Lucy asked. "Did you learn their identity?"

"The usual suspects."

"What the hell does that mean?" John demanded.

Lucy explicated it gently: "I believe, John, that Timothy is referring to the fact that unexplained fires are usually attributed to teenage vandals or homeless derelicts. Just as unexplained murders are always said to be drug-related."

"Exactly," Timothy confirmed.

"Why do you characterize this vehicle as 'strange,' Timothy?"

"It is—or was—a large camper. A mobile motor home."

"Do you know the parking lot?"

"I know where it is."

"Excellent. As my Aunt Hattie always says, 'Keep your ears open at breakfast and your eyes open at supper.'"

"What does one do at lunchtime?" I asked innocently.

There was no response. We were all piling into a cab for a nerve-racking journey to Long Island City.

All during that ride I kept darting glances at Timothy. The young man was beginning to disturb me. He had shown little interest in the whole murderous affair—and then suddenly taken matters into his own hands, without consulting anyone.

With brilliant results, but still . . .

I thought of Lucy's warning. Beware the laughing gull. Perhaps that applied to the young man also. The gull laughs because it can't sing. Maybe Timothy investigates a dead person because he can't deal with a live person. Maybe . . . oh, who knows! As for the warning about the white-eared hummingbird—well, the application of that to Timothy's life was even more obscure.

At the end of the forty-minute drive we were in a wretched parking lot for trucks in an industrial section of Long Island City, surrounded by closed-down factory buildings and a few operating warehouses.

There was only one camper on the lot—a burned-out wreck against the back fence.

As we approached it, a man in a small shed with a rottweiler on a short leash poked his head out and shouted, "Fifty bucks! As is! You cart it!"

Lucy nodded as if she would consider it seriously.

There was no door left on what had obviously once been a substantial motor home.

Timothy entered first. We all followed. The interior was charred and splintered by fire axes. There were muddy puddles on the floor. The walls of the small kitchen were pulled out. The strong odor of burnt plastic and fiberglass made me a bit nauseous.

"Take a look at this!" John Wu called out. We milled about him and the small control panel, scorched black, set over what had once been a sofa built into the wall of the camper.

"It's just the interior temperature controls," I said, noting the heat and air-conditioner adjustments.

"More than that!" John rebuked. "Look here. A gauge for pollen count. And humidity. Pretty high tech for a simple camper."

"Maybe it was a bordello," suggested Isobel.

"What does the pollen count have to do with a bordello?" John asked angrily.

"You'd be surprised," she answered mysteriously.

We walked on, toward the rear of the mobile home, opening the narrow closets high along each side of the vehicle.

The first one I opened was filled with charred clothes.

The second one rained a shower of junk down on me. I stepped back, realizing it was strange junk indeed . . . small aluminum foil-covered cylinders.

John Wu picked one up.

"Like baking squash in a stove," he said as an explanation why the objects were relatively intact after the fire.

Timothy picked one up and undid the aluminum wrapping. Underneath was an ordinary cylindrical mailing tube.

We unwrapped others. All the same.

"Maybe she was also in the saltwater taffy business," suggested Isobel. "Maybe she shipped the taffy in these tubes. And the aluminum kept it chewy."

No one had a more rational explanation. I kicked the tubes out of the aisle and we moved on, but there was nothing else to find.

We headed out of the camper and across the lot.

John gave Timothy a little dig. "Well, I always wanted to spend a morning in a Long Island City truck lot."

Suddenly I realized that Lucy wasn't with us. She must have stayed behind in the trailer.

"Wait for us at the gate," I told the others, and rushed back inside, fearful that she was in some sort of distress.

Yes, there was Lucy. But distress? No. She was leaning against a wall, holding one of the foil-covered tubes. She kept bouncing it delicately in her palm.

"What are you doing, Lucy?"

"Musing."

"They're waiting for us."

She didn't reply. She dropped the tube on the heap.

"Are you musing on the tube's significance? If it has any? And to whom?"

"Actually, Markus, I'm simply musing on what musing is all about."

"You lost me, Lucy."

She threw back her head and laughed . . . a wild wonderful laugh. Was that the way she sounded years ago, in Chapel Hill, when Buford was her lover? My heart accelerated. My hopes soared. Only to be dashed.

"What time is it, Markus?"

"Near eleven."

"When we get back to Manhattan, dear, I would like you to accompany me on my visit to Armand Gratia."

"But I've told you, dear Lucy. The police have already put him through the ringer. He's as clean as a new beach blanket. The man had nothing to do with the murder of Teresa Aguilar. And I'm sure he didn't participate in the construction of that fantastic conspiratorial web you conjured up . . . which is garroting poor Peter."

"Yes, I recall your telling me that. By the way,

how are you using the word 'fantastic'? In the sense that it is very powerful and cruel? Or in the sense that it is fallacious, nonexistent—a fantasy?"

"I'll have to think how I was using it."

"Yes, do that. And while you're thinking, may I remind you that bullfrogs have been known to eat hummingbirds."

Hmmm.

Chapter 9

We found Dr. Armand Gratia that afternoon in a network of tiny offices in a renovated brownstone two blocks from the U.N.

His Mercy Village was only one of what seemed to be at least a dozen rescue-type medical relief missions represented there—including the famous Doctors Without Borders. Three of the latter, I recalled, had just been murdered by dissident elements in Chechnya. They had been French nationals.

As for Mercy Village, I had never heard of it.

And as for Dr. Gratia, he wasn't wearing his signature beret and he didn't seem at all shy. He was a thin, wiry, dark-complexioned, and very handsome man of about forty. I decided he probably came from Belize. Don't ask me why. His English was accented but excellent.

He was wearing a white shirt with open collar and several pens jutted out of his breast pocket. His brilliant black hair, with an almost bluish tint, was combed flat. The thin part looked like a white scar looking for help.

As handsome as he was, there was a jarring note—the excessively delicate, fine-boned face. Maybe that was why Helen Bells, the boutique owner, thought him shy.

"We are friends of the man who was to marry Teresa Aguilar," Lucy announced.

He stared at her with a kind of astonished curiosity. Behind him, on the walls, was a riot of humanitarian posters. Ten feet away was another desk at which two severe-looking women were fiddling with a fax machine.

He didn't respond—not verbally, anyway.

"Did you hear me?" Lucy asked, a bit testily.

"Yes, I heard you."

"I have a few questions for you."

"Concerning what?"

"Concerning Teresa Aguilar."

He held up a hand. "I answer no questions for strangers. It would be obscene. She was a woman I admired and loved. It was a terrible thing. It calls out for silence. And who are you? Why should I say a word to you? Who cares what you want to know?"

He glared at Lucy, then at me. I could see that his hands had begun to tremble.

"You talk to strangers all the time, Dr. Gratia."

"Yes, but they are ill. And that is Africa. This is here."

"You've just come back, haven't you?"

"Yes."

"From where, specifically?"

"From Zaire, Cameroons, Gabon."

Lucy looked pained.

"Oh, I get so confused with those names. Has Zaire become the Congo or the Congo Republic?"

"The new leaders in Zaire changed it back to the Congo. The Congo Republic is west of old Zaire."

"Thank you for clearing that up. Listen to me, Dr. Gratia. I can't really fault you for your silence in this matter. It must have been very painful for all who loved Teresa Aguilar. To have been murdered like that . . . a bride . . . shot to death in the sunlight in front of an open Bible . . . oh . . . it was a horror. I respect your wishes, Dr. Gratia. Believe me, I have the highest regard for you and your organization. And Africa is a place I have always yearned to go."

This was news to me.

"Many people are obsessed with that continent," the doctor said. "Many people spend their lives dreaming of Africa and never get there."

"My father's stepbrother went to Africa a long time ago," Lucy said.

This, I never knew, either.

"To German Southwest Africa," she added.

"Namibia," corrected Armand Gratia.

"Yes. Of course. Anyway, he went there for gold."

"And did he find it?"

"No. He found a lot of things, I hear. But not gold. And he never came back."

A strange, faraway look shrouded her eyes. Standing there, still in her birding outfit, Lucy Wayles took your breath away. On her, age was a balm.

Then she asked, "Do you know that silly song, Dr. Gratia—'Mother Africa'? A reggae song, I believe."

"Yes."

"Oh, don't get me wrong. I don't mean silly in a pejorative sense. I mean, I want something more."

She sat down on the desk, a strangely informal gesture for Lucy.

"I know what you mean," he said.

She smiled at him. He nodded.

"Yes," she muttered, "Africa. Mother Africa. From whence it all began . . . in Olduvai Gorge."

"I know what you mean," he said again.

"It is a place, I hear, like no other place in the world," she whispered with passion.

He smiled. He folded his hands. He looked at her warmly. She returned the look.

Something was going on. I could tell that. Something strange, not wholesome.

"I can talk for hours about Africa," he said.

"I could listen for hours," she replied.

My God! They were flirting. They were actually flirting with each other. Intensely. I felt very uncomfortable. What was really going on?

"Do you like Senegalese food?" he asked.

She smiled, reached across the desk, and plucked a pen from his pocket. She held it up, turning it around in her hand as if critically inspecting its form and function.

Then she said, "People have noted that I would kill for Senegalese cuisine."

That was a damn lie. But suddenly I understood what was happening.

Lucy and Armand were about to get together. For more than a late lunch.

And she was setting it up in front of me to tell me something!

She was making a fool of me on purpose. She was letting me know beyond any shadow of a doubt that my continued pursuit of her was futile.

Lucy Wayles did not love me and she never would.

The strength seemed to leach out of my body. I thought I would soon collapse.

Then, gathering my courage, I jolted my musculature erect and walked toward the exit.

Lucy came after me and took my arm. I shook her off and kept walking.

"Where are you going, Markus?" she called after me.

"Out of your life. That's what you want . . . isn't it? That's the purpose of this whole charade."

"You're overreacting, dear Markus," she said.

I turned on her in a fury. "Overreacting! You are shameless, Lucy. Do you really think I'm no more than your Cyrano? Your Sancho Panza? Your Dr. Watson? I wanted you for my wife. I wanted you body and soul. I—"

I stopped midsentence, and glared at her. The headband was pulled up from her fine brow. Her blue eyes were both piercing and hurt. Her face was so thin, so lovely, so slightly lined, that I felt a pain in my gut.

Then I said, "Believe me, I get your message, Lucy."

And kept on walking.

I sat on the big old easy chair in my living room, in a stupor of rage, for almost eight hours.

It is not easy for a man my age to have loved so passionately and unrequitedly; and to have lost so brutally and suddenly.

They were grim hours. In retrospect, I believed that I suffered an actual nervous breakdown. And I believe, as strange as it sounds, that it was Duke who pulled me through.

At first I thought he kept paying me visits merely to gloat over my condition. He hobbled in and out of the bedroom; flopped down about five feet from the chair, gave me one of his pit bull stares, rolled over once or twice, and stayed for about five minutes.

I remember that I talked to him in an odd way. I kept repeating several of Lucy's cryptic phrases: Beware the laughing gull. Beware the tufted duck. Beware the butcher bird. Beware the white-eared hummingbird.

Then, when all the "bewares" were used up, he became in a sense my shrink. Then my spiritual adviser. Then my grief counselor. Then just another suffering male I could confide in.

Along about midnight, I drank a whole bottle of German wine and collapsed on my bed, fully clothed. As they used to say in my children's books, "The prince fell into a deep sleep."

The alarm woke me at 6 A.M. I had forgotten to deprogram the object. I jumped up and shut it off.

What am I doing fully clothed? I thought.

I rushed out of bed to begin the customary ablutions preparatory to my departure for Central Park.

Then it hit me. There would be no more Olmsted's Irregulars. No more bird-watching in the park. No more Lucy Wayles. Not for me.

I stripped my crumpled clothes off like a condemned man and showered. Then, zombielike and as naked as the day I was born, I walked into the kitchen and made myself a large mug of sweet black instant espresso.

It tasted like the state of my soul.

The small radio in the kitchen blared out the weather report: it would be one of the hottest days of the year.

Loneliness crept up on me and took me by the throat. Raw, horrible loneliness unrolling for the rest of my natural life. I would be without love, without interests, without friends. Forever. Just a chubby aging man with a three-legged pit bull.

No! I had to fight it. I had to resist that choking fear. I would not be alone. I would live my life.

I stood up in a fury of resolve. But then I simply didn't know what to do. I sat down again, crushed.

Luckily the Goddess of Reason then emerged, perhaps from my toaster, perhaps from the broom closet. At any rate, my many years as a scientist in pursuit of the cure for the common cold kicked in. Reason herself, in all her splendor, spoke to me.

"Markus," she said, "calm down. Yes, you

have lost the woman you love. And yes, you have lost your birding friends. But every day of the week, thousands of others suffer the same shipwrecks and survive. Proceed with your life moderately and modestly. Seek intelligent substitutes, knowing full well that the substitutes will never replace the originals. Remember: There are other people and other groups who will welcome you into their midst."

I knew exactly what she was talking about; the Central Park Bird-watchers, that rather loose aggregate of birders from which the Olmsted's Irregulars had emerged.

Of course they would welcome me back. Why not? They would be happy to have the defector reaffiliate.

I dressed quickly in my birding outfit, slung the navy surplus binoculars over my neck, and taxied to their meeting place in the park, in front of the lake boathouse, twenty blocks south of where the Olmsted's Irregulars met.

No one was there. I was confused. Perhaps I had the gathering time wrong. Perhaps it was the beastly heat, for, unlike the Irregulars, sometimes climate influenced the CPB crew.

"What the hell are you doing here?" a voice boomed out.

I turned. There, on the large rock across the path from the boathouse, sat the bird-watcher Marigold. He was a caustic and difficult man. Rumor had it he used to be a Broadway choreographer. Blond, thin, tall, Marigold was ugly in a serene way, but his conversation was rarely serene.

I greeted him and approached.

"What happened, Markus? The Dragon Lady give you your walking papers?"

He meant Lucy, of course. But I did not protest the insult. It was no longer my job to protect her reputation. Not anymore.

"Something like that," I said mildly, sitting down carefully on the rock.

"You're a bit early but they'll be along soon," he said. Then he added, "Some of them might even be happy to see you. By the way, did you hear of that osprey sighting up at the Harlem Meer?"

"No."

I removed my binoculars and placed them on the rock. Oh, it was warm. How could I have forgotten my hat?

We sat in a kind of brooding silence. Then Marigold gave one of his lip-curling cackles and hooted, "That was wild! Like the Old West."

"What was wild?"

"That shooting. At the park wedding. You should know."

"Oh, that. Well, yes it was wild," I agreed, "and terrifying."

"It's always sad when a bird-watcher gets murdered. I mean, given the state of the world, we're good people."

"No, you have something wrong," I said. "It wasn't Peter Marin who was shot. It was his bride Teresa. Teresa Aguilar."

Marigold looked puzzled. "But she was a bird-watcher as well," he said.

"I never heard that."

"Certainly she was. At least two people have told me they saw her a few times in the Jamaica Bay Wildlife Reserve."

"Really. Are you sure?"

"Of course I'm sure. What's the problem?"

"No problem, Marigold. No problem."

I sat and brooded on that most unexpected bit of information. A worm began to grow in my head. A gnawing speculative worm. It would be fitting if my relationship with Lucy Wayles had ended differently. It would be good for my morale if Lucy realized what she had lost. It would be blessedly ironic if I could suddenly solve the murder of Teresa Aguilar . . . a murder in which all the procedural brilliance of the NYPD and the Olmsted's Irregulars seemed to have wrought absolutely nothing.

I rushed away from a startled Marigold. Once on the street I hailed a cab. The driver had no idea where the Jamaica Bay Wildlife Reserve was. I told him it was on and in Jamaica Bay, Queens, adjacent to JFK Airport. Now he knew.

I tried to relax in the cab but I was too wound up.

Once and only once before I had journeyed— with the Olmsted's Irregulars—to that dense wonderland at the edge of the city; bogside teeming with ducks, terns, egrets, herons, rails, sandpipers, gulls. A cornucopia of trails. A host of birders.

And somewhere within it all, I was now sure, was a man or a woman with a pair of binoculars who knew Teresa Aguilar and the secrets of her life and death.

The cabbie got lost three times. Finally, I was

let out on Cross Bay Boulevard, a quarter of a mile from the entrance.

The day was getting hotter and hotter. It was now hard to breathe.

When I saw the Visitor Center loom up, I veered right and selected the largest of the three trails that presented themselves. I was looking for birders . . . the more the merrier . . . the larger the trail the bigger the bird.

Within moments I was surrounded by high marsh grass and cattails.

The humidity was so dense the flying insects seemed to be moving in slow motion. From time to time I caught a glimpse of Jamaica Bay itself.

For some reason I felt as if I were treading on holy ground—as if Teresa Aguilar herself were right in front of me, ghostly, saintly, leading me on.

A rising jet from the airport brought me back from fantasy with an earsplitting jolt.

My strength was ebbing in the heat, and as my strength ebbed, my construction of speculative scenarios increased.

I was being honored by the mayor, the city council, and the New York police for my brilliant sleuthing. Lucy was at the ceremony. I was polite but distant. She asked me to come back to her and the Irregulars. I demurred. She began to beg. To save her from further embarrassment I promised to call her the next week—if I could find the time.

Then I heard a voice off the trail on my left. Birders? I called out. There was no response.

My clothes were drenched with sweat.

It was not yet ten in the morning but it had to be in excess of ninety degrees. I should have brought water with me, I realized; or some kind of liquid to prevent dehydration.

Another thing began to worry me. Where were the birds? Since I had embarked on the trail I had not seen a single bird of any kind, either stationary or in flight. Was this section of the reserve off-limits to birds for some reason . . . and therefore to birders. No, that didn't make sense. Perhaps, I thought, when the trail moves closer to the bay, as it eventually must, the birds would materialize.

I kept on with my routine. Walk twenty paces and stop. Look, listen, rest. Then twenty paces more.

It was odd that the most important new evidence was discovered by me, and by chance. But why had it remained hidden so long to the police and to Lucy?

And why hadn't Peter Marin mentioned that his bride was a birder?

Maybe Lucy was totally wrong about Peter having met the lovely Teresa in that Sixth Avenue flea market.

Perhaps they had met right here, where I was walking now.

In fact, Peter Marin may not have been caught in a web of circumstance that was destroying him emotionally, financially, or any other way, as Lucy had surmised. Maybe Peter and Teresa were just two ecstatic bird-watchers who had stepped on the wrong toes. Or maybe, just maybe, that long-haired roller-blade killer had no motive at all but a sudden violent hatred. For Cuba? For birders? For brides? For red-bearded men in overalls?

I trudged on, thinking about what John Wu had said—that a truly procedural investigation, from Point A to Point B and beyond, could only be done properly by trained police officers, and that it always turns up unexpected gems.

I chuckled to myself. Markus Bloch was right then the ultimate "proceduralist." Running down clues and tips. Tracking unknown birders in an unknown land to confirm a rumor.

This quest, I knew, would be the final act in that long-running drama called Lucy Wayles and the Olmsted's Irregulars. I mean, the final act with me in the cast. No doubt the show would go on without me.

A sudden stab of longing just to see Lucy forced me to stop. Oh, God, I knew it would be a very long time before I could forget her. I wiped the sweat off my face and neck.

The trail was finally turning toward Jamaica Bay. I tried to walk faster. For the first time I heard the cry of a gull.

I was so completely focused on the sound that I didn't see the young bird-watcher who had stepped out of the high grass and onto the trail until I was about five feet away from him.

"Hello!" I realized I was shouting.

He returned my hello, but very quietly. He was obviously a serious bird-watcher. He had not one, not two, but three pairs of binoculars around his neck, and two seriously expensive cameras and a light meter slung over his shoulder.

"You have no idea how glad I am to see you," I

gushed. Now that I was close up on him, I could see that he was a very young man—perhaps even a boy of less than twenty. He was thin as a rail and apparently had poor eyesight, or at the very least some kind of eye infection, for the corners of both eyes were caked. Probably, I thought, from being out in the sun too much in the Wildlife Reserve. Birding has its costs.

"Did you know a woman who used to come here, a lovely young woman whose name was Teresa Aguilar?" I asked.

"No," he replied. "Do *you* know a woman named Steely Jane?"

"What an unusual name. No," I said. "But I'm not from around here."

"Would you like to meet her?" the young man asked.

"Well," I mumbled, "that would be nice, but I'm rather busy at the moment."

The next thing I knew the young man had a jagged fishing knife in his hand, and the point of it was about an inch away from my Adam's apple.

It was obvious to me that I had made an erroneous identification. The young man was no birder. And it was just as obvious that I was about to be—or perhaps the process had already begun—mugged.

"Just empty all your pockets and throw the stuff on the ground," the boy instructed me.

I did as I was told.

"Now take off your shoes."

I did that too.

He flung the shoes far into the marsh grass. "Put the binoculars on the pile," he then ordered.

"These aren't worth anything," I noted.

"Shut up, old man! You have nothing to say to me."

What happened next was rather inexplicable. There is no doubt in my mind that it was the young man's statement that I had nothing to say to him that drove me into a paroxysm of heroism. I am by nature a gentle soul. But I really dislike being treated as if I am an ignoramus.

Anyway, to make a long story short, as I bent down to deposit the binoculars onto the pile of loot, I gathered every last remaining ounce of my strength and swung the heavy object, aiming for his head.

He, in turn, jabbed at me with his knife. He was going for my throat!

I missed his head and hit him instead in the crotch.

He missed my throat and slashed across the knuckles of my right hand. I fell to the ground then.

That is what happened to me. As for what happened to him—I don't know. Because, as they used to say in adventure novels, ". . . and then everything went black."

Chapter 10

"So this is where you've been hiding."

Those were the first words I heard when I regained full consciousness.

The figure who spoke was blurry at first. But then I realized who it was: Lucy Wayles. She was seated on a chair not five feet from me.

"Where am I?"

"Well, Markus Bloch, it appears you are in a bed in the holding room of Rockaway Hospital emergency ward. According to the head nurse, you have been here for about six hours. You were treated for a knife wound and heat prostration, along with a smidgen of sunstroke. They've given you a sedative. Obviously you had been wandering around without hat or water for a considerable time in a swamp somewhere in Queens."

"You look beautiful," I said, sounding pathetic, I'm sure.

Lucy ignored the comment.

"And it appears, Markus, you had been consorting with criminal types."

"I was mugged, Lucy. Robbed!"

There was skepticism on her face.

My strength came flooding back and with it the hurt. I wanted to blurt out that she and Armand Gratia had also mugged me, in their way. But the sudden realization that I was actually wearing a hospital gown so startled me that I said nothing.

"Drink your juice," Lucy ordered sternly, pointing to the bedside table on which stood a decanter with a glass straw. It was apple juice, and not at all bad. Unfortunately, I picked it up, without thinking, with my right hand. There was pain. I looked down at the monstrously bandaged hand.

"Twenty-one stitches," said Lucy. "But, Markus, it appears that you frightened the criminal so badly that he fled, leaving your possessions intact. That includes your wallet. Which means you have enough cash to escort me back to Manhattan in a taxi. And we must leave now, Markus. There is much to be done."

I was astonished. She was talking as if nothing had happened between the two of us. And she obviously had no inkling why I was wandering in the Jamaica Bay Wildlife Reserve.

I started to tell her what Marigold had disclosed to me about Teresa Aguilar. But she was quick to cut me off.

"You can give a statement to the police by phone tomorrow. Tell them anything you want to tell them. Now, let's get down to business. Do you still have that savings account? With the Home Savings Bank of America, I believe."

"Yes. Of course. But they were taken over by the Greenpoint Savings Bank."

"How much is there in it?"

"Why do you want to know, Lucy?"

"Just answer the question, Markus."

"About sixty-two hundred dollars."

"Can you spare two thousand of it?"

"For what?"

"My, my, Markus Bloch! This incident has made you a mite mistrustful, I'd say. The money is for Peter Marin. We've decided, the Olmsted's

Irregulars, that is, to help Peter out financially—to the extent that we can. And the poor man has finally admitted his plight and realized he needs help. Why, at this very moment, while you are lounging here drinking apple juice, your comrades are at Peter's home, along with some others we invited, for a very exuberant rent party."

She then reached under her chair and pulled out an unsightly pair of rubberized yellow work boots.

"Unfortunately, Markus, your shoes were not found. Put these on and we shall depart."

I was a bit woozy but once out of bed, I functioned quite well. We simply walked right out of the hospital and found a private cab that agreed to take us back to the city for an exorbitant fee.

The moment the cab let us out in front of Peter Marin's dwelling, it was obvious to me that Lucy had not exaggerated. A raucous party did appear to be in progress. The door wasn't even shut.

I saw all the Irregulars when we walked in, along with a great many people I didn't recognize.

Peter seemed in a daze, particularly when someone walked up to him and thrust an envelope into his hand or jacket.

"I'll tell him that your two thousand dollars is forthcoming," Lucy said in a whisper, then she left me all alone. I obtained a cold ale and sat morosely on one of Peter's spinning art director's chairs.

No one evinced the slightest interest in where I had been, what I now knew, or what I had suffered. But how would they know? Lucy didn't seem to be taking anything seriously except the rent party. As for my hand, it no longer ached; it had simply gone numb.

My eyes kept drooping shut. Three or four times the bottle of ale nearly slipped from my fingers.

"You don't seem to be enjoying yourself much," someone said into my left ear. It turned out to be Lucy, who had materialized out of nowhere.

"It's been a long day," I replied.

"I'm going to make it just a bit longer, Markus."

"What do you mean?"

"I need a favor."

"For you? Or for Armand Gratia?" I asked bitterly.

"You seem to be fixated on that man, Markus.

You're getting to be quite the little pit bull. Is it Duke's fault?"

"All right, all right, Lucy. What do you want?"

"Get Peter drunk."

"Are you serious?"

"Yes, Markus, I am."

"But . . . but why?"

"Isobel and I want to go into his burnt-out basement."

"What for?"

"Fun and games, Markus. Buried treasure. That's right. We are going on a treasure hunt. What does it matter now? Don't I deserve some fun?"

"But, Lucy, I don't know how to get anybody drunk."

"Nonsense. Come now. You're a physician—and a man of the world."

I sighed. "What do you suggest?"

"Vodka and cranberry juice. A little intimate conversation. Some more vodka. And then Peter just fades away for a while. Just tuck him in bed. I don't mean for you to get him violently drunk, Markus. Besides, he is halfway to oblivion right now."

I nodded grimly. What else could I do but

agree? Lucy moved off. The party was now on all three floors of the triplex and becoming more crowded and raucous. People seemed to be hanging over the circular staircases that joined the levels. Were these "hangers" Peter's advertising friends?

John Wu waved to me gleefully. I could see Timothy prowling about silently, recording in his mind's eye images that intrigued him. He must have taken the night off from his waiter's job in order to attend this benefit.

Then I caught sight of Peter Marin. He stood alone in front of one of the floor-to-ceiling closets, his hand on the doorknob.

I leapt—more or less—into action, gathering a vodka/cranberry concoction and joining him. He grabbed the drink away from me without my even having to offer it.

"Hard times, eh, Peter?" I noted sympathetically.

"You said it. Oh, well, the bigger they are, the harder they fall. Isn't that the saying, Markus?" He didn't give me time to answer. He just began to chuckle bitterly, adding, "Well, I sure fell."

"Things change, Peter."

He laughed even more derisively, and clapped me on the back so hard that I almost fell down.

"I'll pay everyone back, every penny," he declared, then downed the drink in one motion.

I led him along the wall to the portable bar where I mixed another drink for him. The mixing was damn awkward this time, as my right hand had begun to throb. Peter never even noticed my wound.

"You're being nice to me because you pity me," he said. "Isn't that the lousy truth?"

"No, Peter. Because you're my friend."

He looked at me rather peculiarly. "Are we friends? Really? I doubt it. We look for birds together a few mornings each week, that's all. I *had* a friend. Oh, yes, I had a friend. But I lost her. I had a career. And suddenly styles changed and I lost that too. And you know what else I had? I had a love. And then suddenly, without rhyme or reason, it was blasted into eternity. Eternity may be a beautiful place, Markus. But it's worthless in the here and now, isn't it? Eternity doesn't pay the bills. And you can't hold eternity in your arms at night, now, can you?"

He looked around wildly. "What the hell am I talking about?" he muttered. "Give me a drink."

I pointed to the glass in his hand and watched as he drank from it. "I was wondering, Peter," I said, "did you ever go birding in Jamaica Bay?"

He was taken aback by the question. It took a minute for him to answer. "Once. I went with Lucy and all of you."

"Yes, I know. But I meant did you ever go there with Teresa?"

Peter grunted. "What the—this is damn strange! One of those detectives asked me the same thing. The answer is still no."

He sloshed the ice cubes around in his glass. "What is with all these crazy questions? They asked so many fool questions, and I had no idea what they were talking about. Did I buy Teresa's mobile home for her? Did I know of anyone who had a reason to destroy it? What are they talking about? What mobile home? Teresa lived in a normal apartment, in Sunnyside.

"Then they questioned me about my vacation. Where did I travel? Who did I travel with? How much money did I take and how much did I come back with? I tried to tell them—my 'vacation' consisted of sleeping for twenty-four hours in a midtown hotel, a place on Forty-fifth Street. But they didn't believe me. They had the *gall* to not believe me. And they refused to say why they were asking these incredible things."

He drained the glass and began to gesticulate wildly. "Questions! Answers! Questions! Answers! Like a night heron hunting frogs in murky water. Dip. Dip. Dip."

"Calm yourself, Peter," I implored. I looked up. Lucy was watching from across the room.

I made Peter a final drink, took his arm, and led him to a small alcove near the kitchen. There was a bench there and we both sat down on it.

He kept mumbling inarticulately. It dawned on me that it was possible—even plausible— Peter Marin knew absolutely nothing about the mysterious Teresa Aguilar except that she lived in Sunnyside and made dresses, and that he loved her.

After all, had I known anything about that Buford person?

I felt a sudden pressure on my shoulder. Peter had collapsed on it, his head weighting heavily upon me.

I lifted my bandaged hand in greeting to Lucy. She smiled. At least I think she smiled. Then she vanished from sight.

I continued to keep Peter Marin company. I too dozed off.

Just how long I was out, I don't really know. What roused me were the ice cubes on my face, wielded by Lucy. When I was conscious again, she placed three cubes on Peter's forehead. Still groggy, he tried to brush them away, but Lucy persisted.

When he came around, he was disoriented and not a little grumpy. He was mumbling incoherently.

Lucy signaled that I should take one of his arms; she grasped the other. We pulled, pushed, and dragged the large man down into the ruined basement.

John, Timothy, and Isobel were waiting for us. I had no idea what was going on. The place was a grim low-ceilinged storeroom. The smoke and water damage was extensive. The basement was filled with all manner of once-valuable items: books, drawings, office supplies, furniture, and bric-a-brac. All transformed, thanks to the delinquents and the zealous firemen, into absolute junk.

There were four windows onto the outside below street level—the inebriated kids had obviously used these to enter the premises—but all the glass panes were missing now, replaced by wooden boards.

There was no air-conditioning down there, of course. It was fearsomely hot.

In the center of the room, under a large ceiling fan, probably long out of commission, a space had been cleared. It reminded me of a campsite in the wilderness.

Lucy and I led the confused Peter over to that spot. She pushed him down on an upended box.

Then she picked up some shards from the floor, held them in her open palm, and displayed them to Peter as if they possessed great intrinsic value.

He made a grunting noise, his eyes closed. It was I who began to study the slivers. They looked to me like the shattered remains of old phonograph records, seventy-eights they were called; these were in use before records were made of vinyl.

"There were old phonograph recordings hidden up there in the fan," Lucy confirmed. "That is all that's left of them."

She shoved the shiny black pieces under Peter's nose. "What were they?" she demanded.

"Teresa's records," he answered groggily.

"What kind of records were they?"

"Nature records."

"Be specific, Peter," she commanded.

"Bird song," he said, groaning. "Maybe from the 1930s. Put out by Cornell's Ornithology Department. They did a lot of those bird records in the early days."

"Why would they be kept up there in the fan?" Lucy insisted.

Peter shrugged. "Teresa said she needed a good hiding place for them. She told me they were valuable. I said she could use the basement."

John was laughing openly. "That is utterly ridiculous," he scoffed. "Records like that are completely worthless. Even when they're in mint condition. It doesn't matter what kind of bird song is on them. They're worth nothing, I tell you."

"How can you be so sure of that, John?" asked Lucy.

"It's hotter than hell down here!" Peter complained loudly. He tried getting to his feet, but Lucy pushed him back down.

"I'll get you some more ice in a minute," she promised. "But first let John answer."

"Yes," Isobel put in, "let's hear the wisdom of Wu." She seemed to love to make fun of John and his tendency to make pompous statements.

"Very well," he said sniffily. "Reason number one: those recordings were terrible—technically, I mean. They had to be. The whole process of recording outside a studio in those years was primitive, laborious. There was no such thing as truly portable taping equipment at the time. The people at Cornell used one of those 'elephant ears,' which was a huge dish—"

"A parabolic reflector," Timothy interjected.

"Exactly!" said John. "In the center of the radar-type dish was a microphone. From the dish, wires ran back to a vehicle where the recording equipment was located. You had to set the whole mess up and hope some birds would saunter by and sing for a bit. See? The records produced by those methods were by our current standards less than primitive—they were pathetic. What value could they possibly have now? Besides, hundred of thousands of them were sold. It isn't as though they were the slightest bit rare."

"The sentimental value, perhaps," Lucy suggested.

"Maybe. But hiding them that way, as though they were valuable antiques? It makes no sense."

"Get to reason number two," Isobel ordered.

"Yes," John said. "The second reason should be as plain as . . . as plain as the nose on your face, Isobel. People don't buy bird song records anymore. If they want to hear something like that, they go out and listen for themselves, or maybe even record them for themselves. I don't have a single bird song record, tape, or CD in my apartment—and I'll bet none of you has one either—and we're all frankly passionate bird fanciers."

There was a ruminative silence.

Isobel was the one to break it. "I do agree with your premise, John," she said somewhat wearily, "but not with your conclusion. You go too far. You don't speak for all birders. Surely you don't speak for me. Of course I wouldn't pay a dime for one of those old records. But I did run right out and buy 'All God's Children' about four years ago. It's one of my favorite CDs."

"What," Lucy asked, "is that?"

"One of those Save the Earth fund-raising extravaganzas. Half the proceeds went to groups like Greenpeace. It's just one CD, but on it you can hear humpback whales, wolves, loons, rock bands—a sampling of sounds from all sorts of 'creatures,' shall we say."

"Oh, yes," John said. "I remember that thing."

"So do I," added Timothy.

I had never heard of it. And apparently neither had Lucy. "What type of bird songs are on this recording, other than loons?" she asked.

"No others. Just the loons," Isobel answered. Then she asked coyly, "Isn't that enough?"

"I'd love to hear that CD, Isobel."

"Anytime. We'll make an afternoon of it," she said sarcastically.

"I meant right now, Isobel."

"Oh. Well, it's not exactly something I carry around with me."

"Can you go home for it—bring it here?"

"Now?"

"Yes, dear."

"Whatever for, Lucy?"

"We don't need a reason. People bring records to parties all the time, don't they?"

"But it's hardly something you can dance to," Isobel pointed out.

"We can try."

"All right," said Isobel. "Why not! It might be a hoot at that. Keep my beer cold."

And with that, Isobel scrambled to her feet and dashed out of the basement.

We all rejoined the party, still going strong upstairs.

"No more for him," Lucy whispered to me as we mixed in with the crowd. She meant Peter, I assumed. She was saying he should be kept away from alcohol for the rest of the night.

Isobel returned in forty minutes with the CD. The Irregulars repaired to the third level of the triplex—the music room. It also contained a television set and a short-wave radio. Two other guests, either inebriated or ill, were sprawled across chairs. They took no notice of us.

The CD in its plastic case was circulated among us. Peter glanced at it and handed it to me. I stared at the cover, which showed a humpback whale breaking the water with a celestial halo in the background, then passed the box on to Timothy. He studied it front and back. John hardly glanced at it. But Lucy studied the CD minutely. She read the cover copy, then opened the case and read the little information booklet. Finally she seemed satisfied. She then handed it to Isobel who passed it once again to Peter, pointing to the high-tech console. "Play it, Pete!" she demanded.

Peter made no move to play the CD; he only stared ahead glumly. Timothy snatched it out of his hand and in a series of swift coordinated moves got the disc inserted and the machine up and running.

We all listened. First came the rock band—the Grateful Dead; then the whale songs; next the Harlem Boys Choir; a howling, baying, wild wolf symphony; an Irish folksinger; and then the loons.

The loon songs were mesmerizing, almost impossible to describe. They were part laughter, part moan, part lieder, part lyrical flute. One could immediately understand how the phrase "crazy as a loon" came about. But, believe me, the phrase maligns the bird and its song.

I sat there, utterly transfixed. I'm a cynical city dweller, but those songs pierced my armor and made me tremble with . . . with what? Well, I guess it was just the realization that a loon calling and singing in the cold northern night was like nothing else on earth. Mad? Yes. But also beautiful and eerie and penetrating.

The song ended. Timothy pushed a button and the CD stopped playing.

"Well?" It was Isobel who spoke.

No one said a word.

"I'm speaking to you, John," she said pointedly.

"Yes. I can hear you," he answered finally.

"So? So what do you have to say?"

He turned sheepish. "I didn't know what I was talking about. I definitely would have bought that CD had I known about the loon songs."

Isobel beamed.

"You obviously enjoyed it very much, John," noted Lucy. "Why?"

"Why?" he repeated in disbelief. "Why? Because . . . damn it, Lucy, you know why. I have heard loons before, but never like this. The mix was beautiful. The sound reproduction was wonderful. And they got *all* the calls. Did you notice that? The intimate family conversation . . . the hoots. The raucous territorial yodels. The wailing danger calls . . . the tremolo. Everything! It is an amazing cut. You feel like you're in a canoe on a lake in the Canadian wilderness. You get the same chill."

There were nods of assent all around. Lucy gestured to Timothy to play the selection again.

This second playing seemed even more intense, at least it was for me. It made me wonder if, before I die, I could arrange to have my coffin sunk in a loon lake, so that their songs would echo off the casket forever.

When the cut was over, Lucy said, "Yes. No doubt."

"No doubt about what?" John demanded.

"No doubt they're beautiful sounds," she said. Then she added, "But they're not loons."

A hush descended over the room. We all fell into confused silence, except for Peter, who seemed to have been jolted out of his stupor by Lucy's last statement.

"What are you talking about, Lucy?" asked Isobel.

"I am saying that what we heard was not the common loon, *Gavia immer*."

All hell broke loose. Remonstrations. Demonstrations. Accusations.

A sly smile spread across Lucy's lovely face and she raised her hand, calling for silence.

"My goodness! Cain't y'all city folk take a li'l joke?" she said, laying on the down-home accent.

Feelings were soothed.

Then Lucy announced loudly, "Unfortunately, Markus and I will not be in the park tomorrow morning as usual. I have to take Dr. Bloch to the foot doctor—early. The poor man is suffering something awful. Please carry on without us."

Foot? Feet? Doctor? What was she talking about now? What was Lucy Wayles up to?

But, by then, I was too weary to inquire.

Lucy walked me out to a cab. "You tell Duke," she said, "that I shall be there at seven with a special treat for him."

Chapter 11

Forgive the cliché, but I slept like a dead man that night.

Given the misadventure in the marshes, the mugging, the hospital, the rent party, and the loons—it was, I suppose, inevitable.

Since I wasn't birding the next morning, and since Lucy was due to arrive at seven, I set the alarm for a luxurious six-thirty.

Before I went to bed, however, I did a rather shameful thing. I deposited those horrendous rubberized boots in Duke's room, right on the floor, hoping the felonious ingrate would tear them to pieces as he had done my dress shoes.

The first thing I did when the alarm went off was rush into Duke's bedroom, hoping for the worst. Not to be. The boots were untouched.

"You are a cross to bear," I said to him. He yawned.

Lucy was prompt. And I was ready for her.

The moment the door opened, I demanded in my toughest voice, "What was that nonsense about a foot doctor?"

She kissed me on the forehead. I melted like an iceberg in the Amazon.

"Is the coffee ready, Markus?" she asked.

I rushed into the kitchen to get it done.

The dog ambled out just then.

"Duke!" Lucy exclaimed. "You look wonderful. Is the mean man finally treating you nice?"

From where I stood I could see Duke going into the first part of his act; his ugly face dissolved into a soft grin and his little tail started to flick back and forth.

"I have a stupendous treat for you," Lucy told him. She dropped one of those horsehide chewing bones on the floor in front of him.

Duke went into the second part of his act. He picked up the bone and hobbled about as if he were ecstatic; then he clumped into his bedroom and left the bone on the rug along with the twenty or so other chewables Lucy had brought him since he'd moved in with me. He never touched one of them again once she walked out the door.

Soon he was back in the living room. Time to climb on Lucy's lap as she sat in my favorite chair. He loved to do that.

When I brought the coffee in, he was up there having his ears pulled. On his face was that pit bull grin—cryptic to say the least.

I sat down on the sofa across from them.

"The coffee is excellent, Markus," she said.

As I said "thank you" I noticed for the first time that she was dressed very primly, like a schoolmarm: dark gray skirt and blouse with brown lace-up shoes.

"Are you wide awake?" Lucy asked.

"Of course."

"Then you wouldn't mind if we had a little conversation."

"Mind? I'd welcome it."

"What do you see when you look at me, Markus?"

"I see a beautiful, mature, intelligent woman whom I love very much."

"Is that all?"

"I see a woman who torments me."

"How do I do that?"

"Many ways, Lucy. Like what happened with you and Armand Gratia. And the way you always leave me hanging with those cryptic remarks you make. And the way you go off on your own on wild goose chases. And the way you seem to enjoy making me play the fool in front of others. And the simple fact that you rarely take me into your confidence. And . . ."

I ran out of breath there.

"My, my, that was a mouthful, Markus."

"Well, you did ask."

"Yes, I certainly did."

"What, by the way, was your point in asking?" I said. "Are you going to change your ways?"

"Change my ways? Markus, you're starting to sound like a born-again, foot-washing Baptist."

Duke let himself down from her lap and headed for his bedroom.

"He looks well, Markus," Lucy noted.

"I do my best."

"Yes, you always do. Now why don't you get dressed? We'll go for a stroll. We have a nine o'clock appointment."

"We do? Where? With whom? You don't mean with a foot doctor?"

"Oh, Markus, where did you ever get such a

crazy idea? Your feet are in fine shape for a man of your age."

"Wait just a minute! What was the point of the conversation we just had?"

"Point? You're a wise man, Markus Bloch. Isn't that enough of a reason?"

I dressed quickly and went for a long stroll with her, arm in arm, up and down Fifty-seventh Street.

At 8:55 A.M. she led me to Carnegie Hall.

"Are we going to rehearse?" I quipped.

"Not quite. We're going around the corner to the Carnegie Hall Tower to visit a gentleman named Jon Jerrard."

"And who is he?"

"The president, I imagine, of Jon Jerrard Productions, Inc. The company that produced the CD called 'All God's Children.'"

I had no idea what she was up to. So all I could offer in response was: "I thought pop music promoters operated out of the Brill Building on Broadway—not Carnegie Hall."

"It's a whole new world, Markus."

We walked just around the corner from Carnegie Hall itself. We entered a building and rode to the fourteenth floor. Mr. Jerrard had not yet arrived at work. His secretary, a young and rather gruff-speaking boy, inquired as to the purpose of our visit. Lucy replied that it was "private and urgent."

He regarded us doubtfully but invited us to wait.

We sat down on a two-mile-long leather sofa that was sumptuously smooth. Lucy stared straight ahead. I found and leafed through a copy of a magazine devoted to cigars.

There was an edge to Lucy and it made me nervous.

Jon Jerrard entered at nine-thirty sharp. He was surprised to see people waiting. The secretary briefed him in whispers.

"Give me five minutes," he said to us, and vanished inside his private office. Mr. Jerrard was not what I imagined a pop music promoter would look like. He was dressed more like a field geologist searching for oil, and he was much older than I would have expected.

Finally we were ushered in to his stripped-down, no-nonsense office, where the only hint of clutter consisted of the snarl of wires interconnecting an elaborate PC, copier, phone, and fax setup.

"Now, what can I do for you people? What is this 'private and urgent' business you have with me?"

Despite his words, he seemed quite friendly, even interested. He had a container of coffee and a magnificent chocolate chip muffin on the desk in front of him. My mouth was watering. If asked to, I'd have sat up and begged for half of it, but I managed to maintain my dignity.

"We are here concerning the CD 'All God's Children,' which you produced," said Lucy.

Jerrard laughed. "Don't tell me. Let me guess. You're lawyers."

"No."

"Tax people?"

"No."

"Foundation people? Friends of Animals?"

"No."

He looked perplexed as he bit into his muffin.

"OK. I give up."

"Was that CD a success?" Lucy inquired.

"By any criteria. Beyond our wildest dreams. It sold in the millions. I made money. The artists made money—even after kicking back a bundle. All the participants came out smelling like roses. And that single CD must have funded twenty environmental groups. Everybody walked away happy."

"Including the loons?" Lucy asked.

"Excuse me?"

"One of the selections on your CD featured the singing of loons."

"Yes, that's right. So what?"

"Where did you obtain those loon songs?"

"Why do you want to know that?"

"We're loon lovers."

He chortled. "What do you mean—you think the birds were abused?"

"I mean we're just making inquiries."

The tone of the conversation was subtly turning, becoming decidedly unpleasant.

"How is the muffin?" I asked. "It looks wonderful."

He looked at me as if I were insane. Then he looked over at Lucy, probably attempting to decide whether she was crazy as well.

"OK," he said suddenly. "I guess there's no harm in telling you. I purchased the loon tape for forty thousand dollars."

"From whom?" asked Lucy.

"From a Canadian nun. Sister Elizabeth, she was called. She's from an order in Winnipeg.

Don't remember what they called themselves exactly. Daughters of the Covenant, or something like that. It's been a few years now. Anyway, the sister contacted me."

"How did you find out about this order of nuns?"

"I didn't. I just told you, they contacted *me*. This Sister Elizabeth said she heard about the CD we were putting together, featuring wildlife sounds and big name music groups. She just called me one day."

"Who set the price?"

"For the album, you mean?"

"No. The fee for using the loon songs," Lucy explained. "Who decided that forty thousand dollars was the appropriate amount?"

"She did. Sister Elizabeth. The order supports itself by farming. They needed money to buy farm machinery and land. They taped the birds. I listened to the tape and—Wow! I loved it. It seemed perfect. I paid exactly what she asked for it. That's it."

"And what about royalties from sales of the CD? Does the convent get regular payments?"

"None, of course. The forty thousand was a onetime fee."

"Can you describe this Sister Elizabeth?"

"No. How could I? We never met. All business was transacted by phone."

"I see. Well, Mr. Jerrard, I want to thank you for being so candid," Lucy said. She stood, extended her arm across the desk, shook hands warmly with him, then led me out of the room.

Back on the street, she did not speak. I could see that she had grown rather pale.

"You look shaken, Lucy," I noted. "Now can you tell me what this visit was all about?"

"I'm depressed, Markus. I need a drink. Perhaps a Peter Marin-type drink—something with vodka. Yes, that would be quite nice."

"It's ten o'clock in the morning, Lucy!"

She looked at me directly. "I am aware of the time."

I took her into one of the few bars in the vicinity open at that hour, a small place on Fifty-seventh Street that masquerades as an authentic Irish pub. It was empty except for the bartender restocking the shelves and an old man polishing the tables at the back.

Lucy got her vodka with cranberry juice. I ordered an ascetic club soda with lemon. We sat side by side on bar stools. No sunlight could penetrate the dark windows up near the entrance. We were enveloped by gloom.

"Tell me why you're depressed, Lucy," I pleaded, sorry of course that she was in distress, but also rather thrilled that she might at last unburden herself, take me into her confidence, as I had said earlier.

But no. Her response was, "What a silly question for a physician to ask. The world, perhaps, is too much with me."

"Was it something Jerrard said?" I persisted.

She did not answer. I busied myself with squeezing the lemon.

"Markus, did I ever tell you how I happened to become a bird-watcher?"

"Why, no. I assumed you were born a bird-watcher."

"On the contrary, I had no interest in those creatures at all. Until high school. And it was a poem that did it."

"A poem?"

"Yes. 'Ode to a Nightingale.'"

"Ah yes. Keats. I remember it well."

"Not the entire poem, mind you. Just a few lines—from part seven, if I recall."

"Actually, I don't remember specific lines, Lucy."

In a flash, she was off the bar stool, standing ramrod straight. She began to declaim in melodious, overarticulated tones:

"Thou was not born for death, immortal Bird!
 No hungry generations tread thee down;
 The voice I hear this passing night was heard
 In ancient days by emperor and clown;
 Perhaps the self-same song that found a path
 Through the sad heart of Ruth, when, sick for home,
 She stood in tears amid the alien corn . . ."

There was silence. I stared at her in astonishment. Both bartender and cleaning man were doing the same.

Lucy climbed back on the stool. "Yes, Markus, it was that poem."

"So it appears."

"Perhaps it is time for me to relax my grip, Markus."

"Grip?"

"Maybe John Wu was correct. Without any suspects, the murder of that angelic Teresa Aguilar will never be solved. Except by a single lucky break erupting without rhyme or reason from a long protracted procedural investigation by true professionals."

"That is a mouthful," I noted.

"And perhaps," Lucy continued, "our worry over Peter has been exaggerated, unnecessary even. He seems to be overcoming his grief. He seems to have accepted his financial status and is working hard to get out of the hole he dug for himself."

"Yes," I agreed, "he does seem somewhat better."

"And perhaps our horror at what we witnessed in the park that morning is—how shall I put it?—overblown. There are many horrors in the world more grievous."

"Certainly that's true."

"All right then," she said with resolve. "Yes! I think I shall release my grip. Start anew. You and bird-watching and a good life. That's what the future holds for me, dear Markus."

"Yes! Yes, Lucy!" I wanted to dance in the street, drink champagne from her sneaker, alert the media. "Oh, Lucy, that makes so much *sense!*"

She finished her drink, a smile of contentment

on her lips (nothing compared to the one on my face), and then kissed me lovingly on the cheek.

"Tomorrow, dear?" she said. "At seven. In front of the statue."

"Of course," I said joyfully.

"And you won't forget your binoculars?"

"No, of course not."

"And the moment you leave here you will go to your bank, withdraw two thousand dollars, and send it to Peter."

"Yes, dear."

"Money orders, Markus. Use money orders. Peter gets embarrassed, it seems, when you give him cash."

"A money order it will be."

"What a fine man you are, Markus." And with that she walked out.

I felt there was more than enough cause to celebrate. I ordered my own "Peter Marin-type drink." Then I scurried to the bank. The strange and still unexplained visit to Jon Jerrard's office had already slipped from my mind.

Chapter 12

A brand-new morning. A brand-new day. Life beginning anew. The thrill of the hunt. Wasn't it glorious!

I rushed to the Olmsted's Irregulars meeting place, arriving a full fifteen minutes early.

Timothy was already there, eating an apricot.

So was John Wu, sipping coffee from a paper container.

And so was Lucy, consuming nothing but looking radiant.

In a minute we spotted Peter Marin, ambling toward us. The group applauded his arrival, enthusiastically. It was good to have our Li'l Abner back among us.

Only Isobel was missing. We waited impatiently for her, anxious to get moving. The morning was a bit cloudy, a bit cool, with the sun mischievously peeking in and out—a perfect day for birding.

"There she is," John called out.

He was right. Isobel was coming, but not approaching from her usual direction, and she was carrying several large objects.

"What is all that stuff?" I asked when she joined us, out of breath, and laid her burdens down on the soft dirt of the bridal path.

"What does it look like?" she shot back irritably.

"A video camera. And sound equipment," I answered, feeling cowed.

"Give that man a cigar," she quipped. Then she turned to Lucy. "I have astonishing news," she said in a guarded whisper.

Ears perked, we all gathered around the two of them.

"Early this morning," said Isobel, "I received a call from someone I know quite well. Let's just say this someone is a reputable party. He informed me that several—I repeat—several mountain plovers have been seen in the vicinity of McGuire Air Force Base, in southern New Jersey."

Everyone seemed to catch his breath in a kind of exhalation, or perhaps shock.

I so wanted to be part of the excitement, but I hadn't the foggiest idea why they were all so worked up.

"Yes?" I said to Isobel in expectation. "So . . . ?"

"So? *So?*" she repeated, mocking me. "Do you have any idea how stupid it makes you sound when you say that?"

"Pardon me," I said, blinking.

"That's enough, Isobel," Lucy said. "Let's calm down now. And you, Markus, perhaps you were unaware of, or you've forgotten, that one of the most perplexing avian mysteries known to man is what happens to mountain plovers in August and September. We know where they breed. We know where they winter. But they seem to vanish in between."

"Ah, yes. I did forget," I lied.

"Our duty is clear, I think," Isobel declared.

"Yes," agreed John, "someone must go there."

"Of course. That is why I brought the gear," Isobel said. "Whoever goes has to take it and use it."

"Perhaps we should all go," suggested Lucy.

"Why commit all the troops?" John said. "It

might be a false sighting. That's happened before."

"This source is reputable," Isobel said. "But . . . who knows?"

"Perhaps it would be better if only one of us went," Lucy amended her previous statement.

"That makes more sense," said John.

"Draw lots." The suggestion came from young Timothy.

"No!" Isobel protested. "I think the selection should be made carefully. This is no small assignment. This is a great chance for the Irregulars. It's our chance to make ornithological history."

"That's right," John said, nodding his head vigorously.

"I would suggest choosing the wisest, the bravest, the most adventurous of us," put in Lucy, lifting her head high.

When I looked around at all their faces, every eye was on me. It made me exceedingly nervous. Why were they all looking at me? Had I done something wrong?

Oh.

"Just a minute, Lucy!" I shouted, nearly hysterical.

What was the matter with them—with Lucy? Was she deranged? I might have been the oldest. Yes, sure. But the wisest? The bravest? And as for any affinity between me and these mountain plovers . . . the less said the better.

No! I thought desperately. No, Lucy. No, no, *not* me!

"Well, he is the logical choice," John was saying.

"Hmm," Isobel mused. "Not an inspired choice. But not outside the realm of possibility."

"He's the man," Timothy said with absolute assurance.

"Wait!" I cried out. "All of you—wait. I have no idea how to work that camera. I—I don't know New Jersey at all. I'll get hopelessly lost. And I have never seen a mountain plover in my life."

"Just press the button, Markus," explained Isobel, pointing to the hulking camera.

"Right," Lucy chimed in. "And you do know that area of New Jersey, Markus. It's where you took basic training when you were in the army. Fort Dix."

John took the baton. "It doesn't matter if you've had no experience with mountain plovers, Markus. You'll know it when you see it. Remember: a distinctly swollen bill!"

"Just think of it this way, Markus. It's a shorebird who doesn't like the shore. Instead it likes prairies and grasslands. A peculiar bird. Right up your alley, Markus." So spake Lucy.

I didn't like what was going on. And don't think for a minute I didn't know exactly what that was. They were pulling me in, pulling me deeper. I was being shanghaied. I knew it, but I didn't know how to get out.

"We are bestowing a very high honor on you," John explained. "But remember what it is you're looking for. The plover is a small sandy-colored bird. In the summer, meaning now, it exhibits a white forehead with a small black cap above and a black eyeline below. Can you remember that, Markus?"

Timothy added, "Perhaps it would help you to know that mountain plover females exhibit sequential polyandry during the breeding season."

"And," Isobel reminded me, "they will seek shelter in a prairie dog town—if available."

"All right, Isobel," Lucy said, "do you have the exact location?"

"Of course," she answered, flourishing a piece

of paper and reading aloud from it: "Behind the hangar on runway nine. That is the civilian part of the air base."

"There you have it, Markus. I would suggest a private car service rather than a rental. You need all your strength." Lucy's voice had become brisk now, strictly business.

"Let's call the car service for him," John said.

"Yes, and I'll load the equipment aboard," offered Timothy.

"I am so proud of you!" Lucy exclaimed.

Thus I was railroaded into the mountain plover adventure.

It was a long trip down the spine of New Jersey, on the Turnpike, to Wrightstown and the airport.

My driver didn't make the trip any easier. He was a gloomy, silent Russian émigré who simply didn't answer any of my questions. But he stopped at every rest area along the way for some type of refreshment.

The last half hour of the drive I spent trying to understand the workings of the video camera and the sound attachment.

We found McGuire Air Force Base easily. It was much harder to find the small civilian airport attached to it. The entrance, believe it or not, was through a cornfield.

Finally, a reasonable facsimile of a control tower loomed up and we saw fuel trucks.

The Russian parked the car, leaned back in the seat, and promptly fell asleep. I gathered my equipment and headed for hangar nine, now clearly marked by signs.

As I trudged, I began to experience a glimmer of the excitement surrounding my mission. If indeed I did find and positively identify mountain plovers, I will have made a lasting contribution to the world. That would be more than I accomplished in my thirty-five years as a medical researcher.

My step became springy, my eyes sharp. Yes, in a sense, this was a grand adventure.

As I strode toward hangar nine, I tried to get a picture in my mind of what a mountain plover looked like, assembled from the data given to me by Lucy, Isobel, John, and Timothy.

I reached the hangar. There was activity on the runway. A cargo plane had obviously set down a short time ago. It was a beat-up converted 727. The plane didn't interest me, though. The plover

sighting had been near the hangar, not the runway.

I approached the rear of the dilapidated structure slowly. The terrain around the building was
parched, low-lying grass and shrubs. I hoisted
and adjusted equipment so that it was ready to
shoot.

I slowed my gait deliberately because those
stupid rubberized boots Lucy had given me were
making crunching noises. The poor plovers
would be scared to death.

The sweat was now etched on my face. The
equipment was heavier than I thought. I reached
the structure and began to walk along its perime-
ter. The birds, I knew, would be close to the
building line, using it for shade and shelter.

A raucous bird call suddenly pierced the hot
August air.

Plovers?

I stepped back. The call had come from on
high—like a taunting laugh.

I looked up. No, it was only a bluejay staring
down at me from one of the hangar's corrugated
iron eaves.

I kept on moving. No sign of the plovers, but I
wasn't discouraged. I had the strange sense that

they were there . . . waiting . . . yearning to be discovered.

I reached the front of the hangar and walked quickly past the open bay to get to the other side.

Someone shouted. I looked up. A man beside the plane was gesturing to me. I couldn't hear what he was saying, though.

He walked toward me quickly. Now I could hear him.

"Are you from the TV station? Are you the reporter?"

I shook my head no. The man stared at me. Two younger men, closer to the aircraft, were also looking at me.

For the first time I took a good, careful look at that plane. On its nose was painted the name Sister Elizabeth.

What a peculiar name for a plane.

Then I looked at the man who had asked if I was the television reporter. There was something peculiar about him as well.

I walked a few steps closer to him. But he only took the same number of steps back.

My God! I knew this man. It was Armand Gratia. Clearly he had recognized me at the same moment.

He did a funny thing then. He whirled around and began shouting to the other men: "Take it up! Take it up!"

In response, they began to run toward the plane's loading chute.

Then, from out of nowhere there appeared two screeching, horn-blowing vehicles. They were heading toward us at top speed.

The four of us—Armand, I, and the two young men—all froze in fear. The vehicles were coming for us like arrows at a bull's-eye.

But then they braked to a screaming stop inches in front of the plane. The lead vehicle was a New Jersey State Trooper highway cruiser. Out of it stepped two troopers in full regalia, their weapons drawn.

From the other car emerged two men and two women.

I could not believe my eyes. The men were Detectives Rupp and Halkin. The two women, Lucy and Isobel—my birding colleagues.

"Hello, Markus," Lucy greeted me, taking my arm and guiding me toward the plane, equipment and all.

We stopped in front of one of the frightened

young fellows. "Does he look familiar?" Lucy asked me.

I looked at him closely. "No."

She jerked the baseball cap from the young man's head and a shock of long golden hair tumbled out.

"Roller blader!" I shouted accusingly. "It's him. The roller blader from Peter's wedding!"

"So it is, Markus, so it is. He is Armand Gratia's son."

Gratia was now shouting at his two cohorts: "Say nothing! Do you understand? Say nothing! This is an illegal search."

"Spot any plovers?" Isobel whispered maliciously into my ear.

I had no answer. My right hand was beginning to ache. I dropped the video and sound equipment right onto the ground.

One of the troopers and one of the detectives climbed the ramp. Lucy, Isobel, and I followed.

The cargo area was dark and musty. Anchored to the walls were crates of X-ray machines and other medical equipment. Even in the gloom I could make out the stenciled letters on the crates: PROPERTY OF MERCY VILLAGE.

We walked toward the tail of the plane.

Suddenly the silence was broken by shouts. "Say nothing! Say nothing!"

I didn't get it. Armand Gratia, who had screamed those very words a few minutes ago, was outside the plane. But those shouts were clearly coming from inside.

Then, what seemed to be a hundred voices began shouting . . . chanting . . . bellowing . . . screeching: *"Say nothing! Say nothing! Illegal search! Illegal search!"*

"There!" Lucy called out, pointing.

On the far side of the plane was a huge thin mesh net hanging from floor to ceiling like a tapestry. We rushed over to it.

Behind the net, anchored to the wall of the plane, must have been a hundred aluminum perches, each one with a small water and food bowl attached.

And on each perch was an identical small, strangely shaped bird. The feathers of each creature were blue-gray and very beautiful. The beak was parrotlike and the tail was red.

"Well, Markus," Lucy said, "you didn't solve the mystery of the mountain plover, but you have just shut down *the* largest smuggling operation dealing in young specimens of the African gray parrot—one of the rarest and certainly the most accomplished talking parrot in the world."

"Illegal search! Illegal search!"

They had all picked up the chant, punctuating it with whistles, taunts, groans, screams of all kinds.

"Shut them up!" cried out the state trooper. "For God's sake, how do you shut them up?"

We were seated on the grass in the shade of the hangar, Lucy, Isobel, and I. The two of them were chattering away. I was still in a state of shock.

"It's going to be a very hot day," Isobel noted.

"Yes," Lucy said, then turned to me and gave me a nice pat on the head. "How do you feel, Markus?"

"Confused."

"Perhaps I can help."

"I would hope so."

"Would you like to hear it from the beginning—my reconstruction of the entire criminal conspiracy? Or would you prefer just the logic of the crime?"

"The former, I think. If it's not too much bother."

"Yes, I thought you would prefer that. But you

must understand that a great deal is still speculative."

"I understand."

"And you must understand that we are dealing with good people who embraced crime to further noble ends."

"I understand."

"Good. Let me begin then. Armand Gratia was, in a sense, a secular saint. He, his wife, and their two sons created and ran Mercy Village. The wife and sons are, for the most part, based in Africa. Armand commutes, raising funds and administering the relief effort from New York. While Mercy Village is under the umbrella of WHO, his funds come only from private charities—religious and otherwise.

"Several years ago Armand began to supplement those funds with what were probably pathetic smuggling efforts—bringing into the U.S. individual gray parrots on his flights back from Africa. He probably sold them for between two thousand and four thousand dollars apiece. No doubt he was troubled by his criminal behavior. And no doubt he persuaded himself that it was justified for the greater good of suffering mankind.

"Then Armand met and fell in love with Teresa Aguilar. She was fascinated by birds. She even owned and listened to old bird song recordings. He told her about the smuggling. She sympathized with his predicament very strongly.

"Together they hatched the loon plan. As everyone knows, gray parrots are astonishing mimics. Teresa played her old records for Armand's smuggled parrots. The birds took to the loon songs with particular fervor and their mimicry was far superior to the original recording. The tape of their loon imitations was sold to the CD producer for forty thousand dollars. Teresa and Armand used the money to lease a plane in order to smuggle in quantity and put Mercy Village on a sound footing.

"Teresa used the nom de guerre Sister Elizabeth when negotiating with the producer. The plane was named in her honor. A mobile home was also purchased to distribute the birds nationwide.

"Alas, the love affair ended. Teresa met Peter and fell in love with him. Now, Peter of course was failing financially. His bubble had burst. People honored his past work but no one was interested in hiring him anymore. He was passé.

"Teresa, in an attempt to help Peter, just as she had helped her former lover, began to extort money from Armand Gratia. She threatened him with disclosure if he didn't kick back to her a percentage of the parrot-smuggling profits.

"I'm sure Armand did kick back money for a while. Then he decided to remove the extortion threat. He flew to Africa so he would not be suspect. His oldest son was flown to the U.S. to assassinate Teresa. He did so. Then he destroyed items that would tie Teresa to his father and the smuggling operation: the old bird records given to Peter for safekeeping and the camper which transported the birds.

"So, you see, Markus, Armand Gratia and his family transformed themselves in a very short time from good samaritans to bloody pirates. It is as simple—and as ugly—as that."

For the longest time, I did not speak. Isobel was silent too, lighting cigarettes and blowing the smoke skyward.

Finally I murmured sourly, "That is one of the most fanciful tales I have ever heard, Lucy."

"Fanciful? I don't think so. I think within a few days Armand Gratia will confirm virtually everything I told you. He knows the game is up.

He is going to tell all, with only a few twists to lessen the criminal charges against his son. He'll try, I think, to claim he pulled the trigger, not the boy. He wants the murder rap. The smuggling charges are minor. You don't do a lot of prison time for breaking quarantine and quota laws on parrots. Oh, yes, Markus. His confession will confirm what I've told you. Besides, all the evidence points to the scenario I just laid out."

I exploded then. "Evidence! What evidence? Where? What about the plovers? How did you know about the plane? What the hell is going on?"

"Calm down, Markus. There's no need for profanity. The plovers, I am afraid, were a ruse. As for the plane, well, it is a bit complex. I had Isobel call Armand. She posed as a TV newsperson wanting to do a story on Mercy Village's work in the war-torn Congo. Armand jumped at the chance. In his field, publicity means funds. He said the Mercy Village plane from Africa was due to land this morning. Isobel arranged to meet him. We sent you because he knew you. We figured he would panic and try to get the plane airborne without control tower clearance. That is, *prima facie* proof of contraband on board. We boarded her and found that contraband. As for the evidence—ah, Markus—it was extensive. If it wasn't, why would the NYPD send two fine detectives down here with us? And state troopers? But I understand your perplexity. Let me give you a quick rundown—a résumé, if you will."

"No! Not quick, Lucy! Go slow."

"Very well. First of all, my inquiries disclosed that there was no music concert in the park on the night Peter's basement was torched. Second, the small tubes we found in Teresa's torched camper are rather standard equipment for those who smuggle exotic birds."

"You never told me that."

"You never asked, Markus. May I continue? Third, there is no order of nuns in Winnipeg, Canada, going by any name remotely like Sisters of the Covenant, and hence no Sister Elizabeth. Fourth, no loons have ever maintained such a lengthy medley of their entire vocal repertoire—not in the wilderness and not in captivity. That tape was either doctored, faked, or some other creature mimicking the loon. It seemed to me the latter, because of the soft whistling in the background. Fifth, if mimicked, only one bird in creation is capable of such mimicry: the African gray parrot."

I could not respond. I felt like a total idiot.

"There were other nuances, Markus. Nuances that I picked up in rather fascinating, rather elliptical conversations with both Peter and Armand. Such as—"

"Enough for the moment, Lucy," I said, watching the troopers and the detectives bundling the cuffed trio into a vehicle.

Other vehicles were pulling up; I assumed to take charge of the contraband. All one hundred or so of them.

"What wonderful creatures they are," said Isobel. "I hear there was a gray parrot in Columbus, Ohio, who had a vocabulary of more than six hundred words. That is enough to write a novel."

Lucy offered: "I like the story of the gray parrot who used to ride in the backseat of an old woman's car. The moment the vehicle entered a town, the parrot would mimic fire engines with such verisimilitude that he created huge traffic jams."

"But the mountain plovers," I protested, unable to let go.

"Forget about them!" yelled Isobel.

It wasn't easy. I brooded all the way back in the private car, flanked by Lucy and Isobel.

At the last rest stop before Manhattan, Lucy and I were left alone in the vehicle for a few moments.

She said, "Tonight, Markus, we celebrate. Please pick me up at seven. We shall dine in a glorious place."

"Anything you say, Lucy."

"And please dress for dinner," she added.

I showered. I slept. I put on my best (and only) summer suit, enhanced by a soft pastel shirt and silk tie. I showed up at Lucy's apartment at the stroke of seven.

She took my breath away, wearing an off-the-shoulder gown as if we were going to a wedding at the Plaza.

We hailed a cab on Fifth Avenue. Lucy told the driver: "Houston and MacDougal." This confused me. What was down there?

"Have you recovered, Markus?" she asked as the cab headed downtown.

An awful lot had happened lately. There were

any number of things Lucy might have been referring to. "Recovered from what?"

"From the excitement of the chase. From the successful denouement."

"I am at ease."

"And you are no longer bitter about the plover ruse?"

"Hardly."

"Excellent. We'll have a good dinner."

Traffic was heavy and the ride downtown was slow. Lucy hummed. I rested.

When the cab dropped us off, we walked half a block toward Prince Street and stopped in front of a small vegetarian restaurant.

"Is *this* the place?" I asked, incredulous. True enough, it featured a kind of nouvelle vegetarian cuisine, and yes, I suppose it could be characterized as upscale, but surely it didn't warrant the kind of dressing up we had done.

"What's the matter, Markus?" she asked. "Don't you like it?"

"It's all right, but . . ."

"Don't you want to eat at the restaurant where Timothy works?"

"Really? This is it?"

"It is."

"Are you sure?"

"Yes, I am. Of course, he didn't tell me where he worked. You know how secretive the young man is. But I'm certain, anyway."

"Why?"

"A simple process of demystification, Markus. We know he's serious about food. We know he works nights as a waiter. In this neighborhood. We know he's basically a frugivore."

"A what?"

"A frugivore. He subsists primarily on fruit, supplemented with grains and occasional junk-food bouts."

"I suppose your logic is sound."

"So I reasoned that he would be working at a fairly fancy downtown vegetarian or so-called health food restaurant. It's a big city, Markus, but there are only five such establishments south of Fourteenth Street. I called them all. This one confirmed that Timothy works here."

We walked inside. Only one table was taken. A hostess, pale and terribly thin, silently seated us.

"I don't see him," I said, looking around the room.

"You won't. He's off tonight," she said.

"Then what are we doing here?" I asked in exasperation.

"Calm down, Markus. I'm sure there are other fine young waiters in this establishment."

"Good evening." The voice behind my right shoulder was deep and resonant. "Would you like to hear our specials this evening?"

I looked up as the waiter came into view.

What I saw jolted me upright in my chair. The alarm bells started going off in my extremities.

The waiter finished his spiel and sauntered off, promising to return in a moment.

"What's the matter, dear? You look ill," said Lucy.

"You know damn well what the matter is, Lucy. That is the young man who showed up at the wedding with the champagne."

She smiled. "I do believe you're right."

"What do we do?"

"Nothing."

"Nothing?"

"Absolutely nothing."

"But, Lucy, what if he recognizes us?"

"Oh, he won't, Markus. Not the way we're dressed now. He saw us only briefly and we were in our birding clothes."

"You knew he would be here?"

"Let us say, I surmised it."

"But how?"

"Remember when you were young, Markus, how you liked to make gallant, romantic gestures under the cloak of anonymity? Surely you do. Anyway, I thought about that young man who so miraculously appeared at the wedding. And I realized that our Timothy, being young, imaginative, and kindly, might have orchestrated it. I thought he would, perhaps, have asked a coworker to perform the gallant task. And when it turned out badly—when the shooting happened—he would not inform on his friend, who had simply done what was asked of him and was not at all implicated in the tragedy. That's what I speculated."

"Interesting," I commented lamely.

She continued, inspecting a spoon as she did so, "My speculations were encouraged when Timothy, with great bravery and at considerable inconvenience to himself, went undercover in Sunnyside to help us in the investigation. It dawned on me that he did this in part to assuage his conscience. He couldn't disclose that he had asked a coworker to come to the wedding with champagne because he didn't want the kindly coworker to be involved in a murder investigation. So he tried to atone for his silence some other way. Yes, our Timothy is a fine young man."

I cringed when the waiter returned.

"Act normal," Lucy cautioned me.

It was Lucy who asked the young man, "Do you serve champagne?"

He replied without blinking an eye, "We serve no alcohol at all."

"Isn't that interesting?" Lucy replied, a trifle loudly, I thought.

The waiter did not respond. We gave him our orders and he delivered them to the kitchen.

I intoned to my companion: "Beware of the laughing gull, Lucy."

She arched an eyebrow. "What does that mean, Markus?"

"It means, she laughs because she's interested in sequential polyandry."

"Markus, dear," she replied, being the slightest bit flirtatious, "I do believe you are twitting me." And then she actually blushed.

I had ordered, by the way, a dish that consisted of four decapitated ultra-ripe tomatoes stuffed with herbed rice and situated within the confines of half a North African eggplant that had been baked in honey from the hives of African killer bees.

I have nothing further to say at this time.

**If you enjoyed this
Lucy Wayles mystery,
be sure to read the
other two books in the
Lucy Wayles series . . .**

BEWARE THE TUFTED DUCK

Always ready to save a bird in need, transplanted Southerner Lucy Wayles rescues a tufted duck from Manhattan's Fifty-ninth Street Bridge. Unfortunately, her arrest for blocking traffic ruffles some feathers among the Central Park Bird-watchers and gets her ousted from the club's presidency. Undaunted, Lucy has formed a new group, Olmsted's Irregulars. But does bad blood between the clubs lead to the slashing death of a rotund bird-watcher Abraham Lescalles? Abraham's money is gone, but so are his old birding shoes. Overlooking this crucial piece of evidence, the police can't see the forest for the trees, and Lucy feels obligated to step in. But the killer's chilling motive can cook her goose . . . if she forgets that fowl play may be deadly.

BEWARE THE BUTCHER BIRD

Lucy Wayles, the feisty leader of the birding group called Olmsted's Irregulars, can distinguish a hairy woodpecker from a yellow-bellied sapsucker. And she doesn't need binoculars to spot murder when she sees it.

When she and the quirky members of the Irregulars arrive at an award dinner for John Wesley Carbondale, the great illustrator of field guides, they are just in time to see Carbondale plummet from the hotel's upper floors onto a hot dog vendor's umbrella. The police call the swan dive a suicide. But Lucy, remembering the butcher bird, which impales its prey on thorns, calls it fowl play. The fact that no one believes her only eggs her on. Now she's hatching a scheme to catch Carbondale's killer, but if her plan goes south, she runs the risk of ending up deader than a dodo.

A new treat for animal lovers . . .

Don't Miss a
Purr-fect Cat Caper in the Next

Alice Nestleton Mystery

by Lydia Adamson

A CAT OF ONE'S OWN

Coming from Dutton
in November 1998

I WAS BLOWING a good-bye kiss to the cats and fishing keys from my purse when the telephone rang.

The whisky-thick voice of my old friend Amanda Avery greeted me. All she said was, "Alice. He's gone."

"Gone? Who's gone?"

"Jake."

"What do you mean, Amanda?" I asked, trying not to sound annoyed.

"Just what I said. My cat vanished. When I got up this morning he was gone."

"Did you leave any of the windows or doors open?"

"No!"

"Then he isn't 'gone,' Amanda. He's only hiding. He's probably sleeping in a closet or behind a desk somewhere."

"No, he isn't. I checked. I've looked everywhere for him." Her voice had become tremulous.

"Don't be silly, Amanda. Cats can find all kinds of strange places to hide. He'll come out as soon as he gets hungry."

The dam broke then. She was crying inconsolably,

muttering incoherently about her late husband; how her life had gone wrong and would never be good again.

I realized I'd better get over there.

"Just hang on, Amanda. Wait for me. I'll come and find Jake for you."

I called my on-again, off-again boyfriend Tony and told him I'd meet him at Pal Joey, adding that I'd be a little late.

Then I rushed out, hopped a cab, and sped to Amanda's place.

The man who answered her door was about forty, very thin, with a bushy mane of reddish hair. He was wearing a gray gym outfit.

"I'm a friend of Amanda's," he said in answer to my unspoken question. "Harvey Stith. I live just up the block. She called me. Sounded if as she was cracking up."

Harvey Stith! "*The* Harvey Stith?" I asked, shaking his proffered hand awkwardly.

"Well, I suppose so. I didn't think anyone remembered my name," he said shyly and chuckled.

He was wrong—*I* remembered his name. Stith had been one of those meteoric *Wunderkinds* who exploded onto Broadway in the early 1980s. Singer, dancer, song writer, director—you name it, he did it.

But then the bubble burst. I heard he had forsaken the commercial theater and accepted a position as director of one of those ambitious graduate programs in theater arts at a California university.

He ushered me in. Poor Amanda, the phone still in

her lap, was on the rug beside her Gordon setter, Good Girl. Two more sorrowful creatures I had never seen.

I looked around the apartment, more critically this time. It had many nooks and crannies, many bookcases and shelves and cabinets and obviously many closets. That two-colored cat, Jake, could be anywhere.

"Stay where you are, Amanda," I told her. "Harvey and I will find him. All you have to do is tell us which closets have trunks or cartons or hat boxes without a lid—that kind of stuff."

She pointed to the hallway.

"Jake-O!" I called. "Come out come out wherever you are." I then commenced my search, opening the closet door. Inside were enough boxes for a flock of shy cats to hide in for a week.

Even with my head inside the closet, I could hear the telephone ring. I wondered if Amanda had made hysterical phone calls to everyone she knew, asking for their help in finding the cat. "Jake-O!" I continued to call. "You come out here this minute!"

It wasn't the cat whose shrill cry I heard. It was Amanda's—she was screaming into the receiver: "But how . . . *How?!* The banks are closed today!"

I walked quickly back to the living room and again looked to Harvey Stith for an answer. He only shrugged.

Amanda hung up abruptly.

She was on her feet by then, shaking, her face bloodless. "He said he has Jake," she announced in a monotone. "He said he wants fifteen thousand dollars or I'll never see Jake again. He said he'd call back in twenty minutes."

"Is this some kind of joke, Amanda?" I asked.

She didn't answer. She knelt beside Good Girl and pulled at one of her ears.

"Something tells me it isn't a joke," Harvey Stith said.

"This man who called," I said, "do you know him, Amanda?"

She shook her head vehemently.

"Are you sure that's what he said? That he wanted $15,000 for Jake."

"Fifteen thousand," she repeated. "If I want him back. He'll call again in twenty minutes." And she began to giggle.

Oh Lord, I thought, she's going to lose control altogether. Harvey and I got her up and led her to a chair. She was tense as a trip wire, fighting panic.

"How could this person have gotten Jake?" she whispered. "How did he get in? When?"

"Call the police, Amanda," Harvey urged.

"No! No police! I want Jake back!"

"But this is insane. Fifteen thousand? You can't just give this man fifteen thousand dollars for an animal you've had for only a few days—a stray from a shelter."

Amanda looked up at me beseechingly. "What would you do, Alice?"

I couldn't answer. I didn't have fifteen thousand dollars. If someone kidnapped one of my cats and demanded a ransom for his safe return, I'd pay anything. But it wasn't for me to say what Amanda should do. The whole thing was so strange. More than just strange, it was unreal.

"Call the police, Amanda," Stith said again. "This is serious business."

"I said no!"

Harvey looked to me for support. But I steadfastly refused to intervene. There were conflicting theories about bringing the police in on kidnappings. Sometimes it worked out for the best; sometimes it ended in tragedy.

We waited in eerie silence.

The apartment became oppressive, as if it were sucking the air out of our lungs. Oddly enough, I could sense the presence of that harlequin cat.

The follow-up call came. Amanda picked up the receiver slowly and brought it to her ear. "Yes . . . Yes," she murmured, and then she fell silent, listening. She did not look at Harvey Stith or at me.

At last she hung up.

"All right. It's set," she told us.

"What's set?" asked Harvey.

"I will go to the bank tomorrow and get the fifteen thousand in twenties and fifties. I'll bring the money to Forty-sixth Street and Twelfth Avenue tomorrow night at ten-thirty. He'll turn Jake over to me and I'll give him the money. I must come alone."

An expression of utter disgust crossed Harvey's face. "This is stupid and dangerous."

"Amanda," I said, "that is a very desolate area at night."

"I don't care. Will you help me—both of you?"

"How?" I asked.

"Just stay close. A block or two away. Then come and collect me and Jake. I know I'll be exhausted and frightened. I won't make it back home by myself."

What choice did we have? Harvey Stith and I made our arrangements: Meet at ten p.m. at the luncheonette on Fifty-seventh Street at Eleventh Avenue. Then go and collect Amanda and, we hoped, Jake.

I went on to brunch at the restaurant. I didn't say a word about what was going on to Tony. It was too difficult to explain—too—well, as I said, unreal.

I spent Monday in a fog of anxiety and indecision. For hours at a time I contemplated the possibility that someone might someday kidnap my own cats.

Several times I felt the urge to phone Amanda and tell her that Harvey Stith was right: the police should be brought in. But I never made that call. Few things in my life I regret more than not making that call.

At nine that evening I took a bus uptown. Harvey was already at the luncheonette when I arrived. We sat glumly in the booth with ripped leather, drinking coffee, not talking at all.

There seemed to be nothing to say. Nothing about our common interest in the theater; nothing about each other's personal life; nothing about Amanda; nothing about Jake the cat, the unfortunate kidnap victim; not even a banal exchange about the weather.

At twenty minutes past ten we began walking toward Twelfth Avenue. The sky was like black velvet—that's how dark it was—and the wind off the water was cutting.

On the avenue now, we turned south, heading for Forty-sixth Street, where Amanda was to meet with the kidnapper.

The piers loomed up on our right. Not a living soul on the street. The only lights came from the truck traffic on the avenue.

At Fiftieth Street, Harvey stopped and squinted at his watch. "We'd better hurry. The exchange should be happening about now," he said.

We picked up our pace, fighting the wind.

Forty-nineth. Forty-eighth. Forty-seventh. No more words exchanged.

"I think I can see her!" he burst out suddenly. "Yes, I see her!"

"Where?" I asked excitedly as we began to run.

"Up ahead, Alice. There! Thank God, she's all right."

Amen, I thought, seeing Amanda for myself then. She was leaning against a No Parking post. Waiting for us. And Jake was all right too, snuggled up against her.

Amanda must have seen us at just about the same moment, because she seemed to be smiling at us. She was waving to us with one hand and holding on tightly to Jake with the other.

Smiling, I said. But that wasn't true.

I was mistaken. That was no smile.

Amanda fell forward, and in that second, Jake leapt clear.

Harvey caught her. The dead weight of her body spun him around and they both went sprawling to the pavement.

Then and only then did I see the ice pick in Amanda's back.